WHAT'S UP, DOC?

What's up? Connecting rooms in a San Francisco hotel, misplaced gems, a $20,000 grant, secret papers, a Chinese dragon and...

What else? Would you believe love?

That's what's up!

Warner Bros.
A Warner Communications Company
presents

BARBRA STREISAND
RYAN O'NEAL

in

WHAT'S UP, DOC?

A Peter Bogdanovich Production

Co-Starring

KENNETH MARS
AUSTIN PENDLETON
SORRELL BOOKE
MICHAEL MURPHY

And introducing
MADELINE KAHN

TECHNICOLOR®

Music Arranged and Conducted by
ARTIE BUTLER

Screenplay by
BUCK HENRY
and
DAVID NEWMAN & ROBERT BENTON

Story by
Peter Bogdanovich

Directed and Produced by
Peter Bogdanovich

"WHAT'S UP, DOC?"

A novel by
Carole Smith

Based on a screenplay by
Buck Henry

From an Original Story by
**David Newman
Robert Benton
Peter Bogdanovich**

 AVON PUBLISHERS OF BARD, CAMELOT, DISCUS AND EQUINOX BOOKS

AVON BOOKS
A division of
The Hearst Corporation
959 Eighth Avenue
New York, New York 10019

First Avon Printing, May, 1972

Printed in the U.S.A.

CHAPTER ONE

This is a story about love and luggage and connecting hotel rooms. In the San Francisco Bristol, to be exact. It is about a Chinese dragon, the Bay, and those fabled San Francisco streets that rise and fall at steep angles all over town. About rocks—some prehistoric specimens and some faceted, expensive gems. About top-secret government documents, a $20,000 grant and mistaken identities. About the people who have the money, the rocks, the jewelry and the documents, and the ones who don't, but want to.

It is also a story about hunger; how's that, you say? *Hunger?* What gives? Or to be more precise, what's up, Doc?

Judy Maxwell was walking. It was a nice day. It felt good and besides, she was broke. Eleven cents in pennies claimed the pocket of her skirt. An overnight case in hand, she whistled between her teeth and cheerfully ignored traffic signals at street corners. Her direction was undetermined; it was a day for drifting. It is good exercise, even slowly walking San Francisco streets. She was getting hungry. With sudden determination she altered her course and headed up a hill. It would come to her, what to do, if she went looking for a solution.

In the San Francisco International Airport, a gray-haired checkroom attendant, wearing a blue drip-dry shirt and navy cap, keeps watch on an overnight case in the middle of the middle shelf to his right. It is in no way out of the ordinary; in fact, it is a match to the one Judy Maxwell carries as she turns a corner and heads north up another hill.

A white tag hangs from the handle of the case in the airport checkroom. When business is light, as it has been on and off this day, the attendant glances at it at intervals of forty-two seconds. When he is busy matching tickets or counting out change, he neglects to do so, but when his work slackens, he looks once again to make sure it is still there. He is a conscientious man.

On a bench nearby, protecting a bag of golf clubs, a man sits. He has been there since early morning. Periodically he stands and stretches and kicks the accumulated cigarette butts at his feet beneath the bench. He is in his mid-forties, graying at the temples and sporting around his middle the paunchy signs of overindulgence. He looks weary; his brown suit jacket is wrinkled in the back; his pants bag slightly at the knees. We will call him Mr. Jones.

And we shall call the man who claims the overnight bag with the white ticket on its handle Mr. Smith.

The attendant tears the ticket from the handle of the case, lifts it from the shelf and carries it to the counter. Mr. Smith hands the man a dollar, takes the case and moves to the end of the counter, sliding it along. The attendant watches out of the corner of his eye as Smith unlocks and opens it.

The case is filled with manila folders. Smith rifles through them quickly. They are clearly stamped Top Secret, in black ink. Satisfied, Mr. Smith closes the case and relocks it. He waits for a woman with two small

8

children in tow to move past, then walks briskly away from the counter.

The checkroom attendant nervously fumbles a large red handkerchief from his pocket, wipes his wet palms and then grandly sweeps it across his forehead. If Mr. Smith had been watching, the movement would have disturbed him. It looked for all the world like a signal.

Which it was.

But Mr. Smith is momentarily distracted by a large woman with a hatbox and a yapping white poodle. She claims the right of way. Mr. Smith gallantly steps aside, then continues walking toward the terminal exit and the rank of taxicabs outside the door. He does not look back. He is a man in his thirties of medium build with hair cut short. He wears moderate sunglasses on the bridge of his ordinary nose. His suit is conservative, gray, rather cheaply made. His shoes need a shine. He melts into any crowd; a man no one would remember. It is an image Smith would like to change.

Mr. Jones grinds out his cigarette, kicks it under the bench, slings the bag of golf clubs over his shoulder, and starts after Smith. It is the overnight case he keeps in sight.

Judy Maxwell turns east. She has had enough of the hill she had been climbing. She has not yet decided on a suitable way to satisfy her hunger. Judy is a particular young woman, and will settle for nothing less than exactly what she wants. She is beginning to tire. The afternoon sun is still warm, although it is at a deep angle now, and will soon set. Her overnight bag seems to have gained weight. She ponders that, and shifts it to her left hand.

The San Francisco International Airport is one of the busiest in the United States, servicing nearly 15,-000,000 travelers a year. The airline terminals, complete with coffee shops, newsstands, shopping arcades and loud-speaker voices floating bodiless over vast spaces, are connected by a hectic maze of roads. People have been known to get lost.

In the terminal being vacated by Mr. Smith and Mr. Jones, a jet has arrived from the Midwest. The passengers have debarked from their plane and now wait before the conveyor belt that will hopefully produce their luggage. In the large main waiting room, at street level, a man steps off the up escalator and walks slowly toward the service booths in the center of the huge room. His name is Howard Bannister. He is in his thirties. He wears glasses, horn-rimmed and appropriate. His tie is vaguely askew. His shirt is white, his jacket striped. He looks around aimlessly, as if wondering where he is to go. He carries an overnight case. It is identical to Judy Maxwell's, and the one with the white tag that has been claimed by Mr. Smith.

Through the large glass doors before him, Howard can see a rank of taxicabs. A man lugging a bag of golf clubs is adjusting himself in the back seat of a cab; he leans forward, gives the driver directions, pulls the door closed behind him, and the cab moves off. Howard looks around, takes a few steps to the right, stops, fingers his chin in consternation and breathes deeply. He wonders what it is that he seems to have forgotten.

Judy Maxwell turns right and sighs at the height of the hill before her. There is nothing to do but go up. She waves at a group of children in a cable car who make faces at her from the window, shifts her overnight bag to her other hand, and gives a little shrug. The noises in her stomach are not yet quite rude, but it is definitely time to eat. She licks her lips, gathers her energy and brightly crosses the street, ignoring the

10

pair of motorcycles barreling down the street toward her. The motorcycles swerve, lose control and tip over on their sides. Judy heads up the hill.

The man in the airport waiting room now stands in the middle of the vast hall. He has stopped fidgeting; his overnight case rests securely on the floor between his feet. His arms hang at his side and he appears to be staring at the arrival/departure board with interest. He is listening to the sounds produced by the flailing heels of a little boy having a tantrum nearby who is kicking the floor despite the protests of his mother.

"Howard! Howard Bannister!"

Howard looks around, surprised. From a terminal corridor marked *Baggage Claims* comes a porter wearing a red cap and pushing a rack containing suitcases. Beside him walks the trim figure of Eunice Burns. It is she who has called. She is wearing the traveling woman's costume—a no-wrinkle double-knit suit. Hers is mint green, with a large collar, decoratively stitched at the seams. Her brown leather pocketbook is firmly clutched beneath her arm, and she carries gloves. She is a sharp-nosed woman, pert and short; her auburn hair is covered with an auburn wig which flips up at the ends. There is the slight sign of a nervous tic above an eye. She is angry.

"Howard, when I ask you to wait for me somewhere, I expect you to stay there until I come back."

Howard nods his head in agreement. "Yes, Eunice."

"It's difficult enough for me to have to see to all these arrangements myself." Eunice gestures with her gloves in the direction of the porter, who has stopped a discreet distance away.

Howard nods his head in agreement. "Yes, Eunice."

She consults her watch. "It's now exactly six-fifteen."

"Yes, Eunice," Howard agrees.

11

"If we reach the Bristol in half an hour, we'll have just enough time to get dressed for the banquet."

Howard nods his head in agreement. "Yes, Eunice."

She turns to the porter, and points to their suitcases. "Put these things in a taxi," she tells him.

The porter nods his head in agreement. "Yes, Eunice." He wheels his cart in a smart about-face and heads for the door. Eunice follows him. Howard stands and watches them go, then looks around regretfully for the little boy, who has finally been calmed by his mother. Eunice starts to say something, looks around, frowns, and returns to place a hand on Howard's elbow. He picks up his overnight case, and they hurry to catch up with the porter.

A taxi has come to a stop at the bottom of one of San Francisco's steeper hills. It is one that Judy Maxwell had half-climbed shortly before. Mr. Smith emerges, carrying his overnight case. Smith pays the driver, the cab pulls away, and he begins climbing the hill.

Another cab comes to a stop at the bottom of the same hill. Mr. Jones wrestles his golf clubs to the curb; he has already paid and well-tipped the driver. He looks at the steepness of the hill before him with mild disgust, allows Smith a reasonable lead, slings the golf bag over his shoulder, and begins the climb. It is hard work. He is out of shape and is soon panting with exertion. Half-way up the hill, Smith unexpectedly turns a corner and Jones is forced to increase his pace to keep up. His face reddens; he shifts the golf bag to his other shoulder. The sun is nearly gone. A slight chill is in the air. When Jones reaches the corner, he gives a sigh of relief. It is a cross street, more or less level; he stands a minute to catch his breath and allow Smith to regain a proper leeway. Once again

12

Jones switches shoulders under the burden of the golf bag, and then resumes walking.

Their suitcases safely stowed, Howard and Eunice settle in the back seat of a taxi for the trip to the Bristol. Howard's overnight case is on the seat between them. He opens it and carefully extracts a large rock. He looks at it affectionately, then taps it with a tuning fork that he takes from his jacket pocket.

"It's a beautiful city, isn't it?" Eunice says.

Howard stares at his rock thoughtfully.

"I'd like to come here on our honeymoon," Eunice continues.

Howard carefully removes a small piece of dust from his rock.

Eunice jabs him none too lightly in the ribs with her elbow. "Did you hear me, Howard? I said I'd like to come here on our honeymoon."

"What? Oh. I thought you wanted to go to *San Francisco* on our honeymoon," he says, bewildered.

Eunice looks at him kindly and says gently, "This *is* San Francisco, Howard."

Howard tears his attention away from his rock and looks out the window. "Oh. Of course it is." With a sigh he settles back in the seat, rock in hand.

Eunice pats him on the arm.

Smith's change of direction is short-lived. At the next corner he turns again and once more Jones hurries to catch up. As he turns the corner he pauses, momentarily in shock at the sight of the long flight of stairs before him. Smith's lead increasing, Jones finally retreats a few steps back around the corner and surreptitiously throws two of his golf clubs into a convenient alley before beginning the climb. Smith holds tightly to his overnight case.

Judy has stopped in front of the large glass window of a pizza parlor, and is hungrily watching the chef

13

prepare the dough for a pizza. Judy's overnight case is on the ground at her feet.

The chef, made nervous by her attention, flips the dough high into the air. Judy watches. The dough does not come down. Slowly the chef lowers his eyes, pursing his lips in anger at Judy. She smiles, takes a last longing look at the finished pizzas on the rack in the window, retrieves her overnight case and continues walking.

A delivery boy with a tray of pastries crosses the street in front of her. Judy watches him for a minute, then with determination she follows, her eyes on the tray.

Mrs. Van Hoskins has completed her buying tour in Haight-Ashbury. Her face is set in an expression of pleasure.

"What time is it, James?"

"Six twenty-five, ma'am," the driver says.

"That late? You had better take me to the Bristol now."

"Yes, ma'am."

Mrs. Van Hoskins settles back into the leather seat of the limousine. A woman in her sixties, the wealthy widow of a successful manipulator of soybean futures, she has spent the hours since her arrival in San Francisco shopping. Her luggage is in the trunk. Her overnight case is on the seat beside her, nearly buried under packages. The car and driver belong to a friend, William Lockland III, whom she will see this evening; he approves of her. Mrs. Van Hoskins wears leopard-skin hot pants and likes to be driven.

Judy Maxwell stands on a corner, her head cocked to one side. On the other side of the street, a block north of where she stands, a man in a brown suit has peered down a side street, retreated a bit down the hill, and thrown a golfclub into a garbage can. She

14

wonders if it could be broken; perhaps it is a putter that has failed him. Never mind. The delivery boy with the tray of pastries has turned a corner; Judy needs to cross the street. She is not watching where she is going. The man with the golfbag has now turned the corner onto the street where she, too, is heading.

There is the screech of brakes. A taxicab has stopped short. In the back seat of the cab, Howard Bannister and Eunice Burns are thrown forward. Howard hits his head hard against the glass partition.

"Owwl!"

"Howard!" Eunice shrieks, leaning forward to help him.

The cabdriver is yelling at Judy. "What are ya' tryin' to do—get yourself killed?"

Judy smiles an apology and continues on her way.

The cabby turns around in the seat, a difficult maneuver with his outstanding stomach. "You all right back there?" he asks.

"I hope nothing's broken," Howard says.

Eunice feels his head with her fingers and looks at it closely. "It's just a bump, Howard. Don't overdramatize."

"No, no," he says. "I mean my igneous rocks." He retrieves his overnight case from the floor where it has fallen. "I hope they're not broken."

"I know how you feel, mister," the cabdriver sympathizes. "I hate it when my igneous rocks are even *touched*."

The cabdriver turns back to the wheel, shaking his head. He waits for a limousine with a woman in the back seat to go past, then drives slowly up the hill, keeping a careful eye out for pedestrians.

CHAPTER TWO

Judy Maxwell has followed the delivery boy and the tray of pastries through a side door of the San Francisco Bristol, and now stands looking at the delivery door through which the pastries have disappeared. Suddenly she has an inspiration. Overnight case in hand, she rides the escalator up to the main floor and winds her way across the lobby to the registration desk. Openly she eyes the mail and key slots, watched by the desk clerk, Fritz.

"Yah, Miss? Can I help you, please?" Fritz asks.

Judy looks at him with a smile. "I was just wondering if some friends of mine were still here," she says. "They're visiting from the . . . ah . . . the New Hebrides," she says brightly. "I believe they're in room seventeen-seventeen."

Fritz looks at the mail slots. He reaches into slot 1717 and takes out two keys. He puts them back.

"I'm sorry, but that room is vacant."

"I don't understand." There is a perplexed note in Judy's voice. "They told me they would be in room seventeen-seventeen of the Hotel Crystal," she explains.

"This is the Bristol, madam," Fritz says stiffly. "Not the Crystal."

16

"Then—one of us must be in the wrong hotel."

Fritz looks nonplused as Judy tosses her head and walks away from the desk. He watches her go. His expression of disdain quickly changes to one of unctuous servility as he turns to see Mrs. Van Hoskins, a long cape over her hot pants outfit, approaching the desk, followed by several bellhops, struggling with luggage and packages. She is a regular customer. He fails to notice Judy Maxwell make an abrupt change of direction and head for the row of house phones out of sight of the desk.

"Ahh, Mrs. Van Hoskins," Fritz says eagerly, bowing. "How nice to have you back with us."

"Thank you, Hans."

"Fritz," Fritz says. "You have your usual room, of course. Seventeen-fifteen."

"Thank you. What happened to Hans?" Mrs. Van Hoskins asks.

"There is no Hans, Mrs. Van Hoskins. There is only me. Fritz."

"Oh—what a shame."

Fritz hastens to get Mrs. Van Hoskins' key from the mail slot. As he does so, she lifts her overnight case and places it on the counter. It is identical to those carried by Smith, Howard Bannister and Judy Maxwell. She opens it. It is jammed with jewelry. She takes off her earrings and puts them carelessly into the case. Fritz turns back with the key and his eyes widen as he sees the jewelry.

"Now, Franz," Mrs. Van Hoskins says, "I'm going to take this case with me now. I need some things for tonight. But tomorrow I will want you to put it in the hotel safe for me."

"It will be done, madam." Fritz looks around for a bellhop; the ones who brought in Mrs. Van Hoskins' luggage have all mysteriously disappeared. "Boy!"

17

Fritz hits the front bell several times. He hands Mrs. Van Hoskins' key to a bellhop, and she follows him to the elevator.

In a chair across the lobby sits the San Francisco Bristol's chunky, middle-aged house dick. His name is Harry. He is reading a newspaper. He does not look up.

Fritz hits the bell several more times.

Harry does not look up.

Fritz hits the bell again, as loudly as he can.

Harry looks up, finally.

Fritz nods his head imperceptibly.

Harry looks at Mrs. Van Hoskins as she walks by carrying her overnight case. He looks back at Fritz and nods.

Fritz nods back.

Harry grimaces and returns to his newspaper.

Judy Maxwell is talking into one of the house phones in the hallway to the left of the main desk. Her voice is low and sensual.

"Hi, room service. This is room seventeen-seventeen." As she speaks, Howard enters the hotel and walks across the lobby to the front desk. Judy watches him with interest as she continues talking into the phone.

"I would like a double-thick roast beef sandwich, medium rare, on rye bread with mustard on the top and mayonnaise on the bottom and a coffee hot-fudge sundae with a large bottle of diet anything."

A waiter, carrying a tray, goes by. Judy reaches out and takes a handful of carrot sticks from a dish on the tray.

"Got that, room service? Yes. Room seventeen-seventeen. Oh, and room service? Would you put it in the hall outside the door. Don't bring it in or knock on the door because I'm just putting my little one to sleep."

18

She hangs up, licks her lips in anticipation, and takes a bite of carrot, her eyes still on Howard, who is now at the registration desk with Eunice.

Fritz has moved to help them.

"I am Miss Eunice Burns and this is my fiance, Dr. Howard Bannister," Eunice tells Fritz. "We're here for the Congress of American Musicologists' Convention."

Fritz checks through the registration cards. Howard is rubbing his head.

"Let me see," Fritz says. He finds the cards. "Burns and Bannister. Here we are. Seventeen-fourteen and seventeen-sixteen. Connecting rooms."

Howard is still rubbing his forehead.

"Howard, go down to the drugstore and get some aspirin," Eunice tells him. "I want you to be in shape for this evening."

A bellhop starts to pick up Howard's overnight case.

"Don't touch that," Howard says quickly. "Those are my pre-Paleozoic tambula rocks."

"Don't touch his rocks," Fritz says sternly.

The bellhop backs off.

"I will take care of those," Eunice says, reaching for the case. "You go to the drugstore and come up to my room in five minutes."

"Right. I'm on my way," Howard says. He walks off a few steps and stops. "Eunice?"

"Yes, Howard?"

"Why am I going to the drugstore?" There is a puzzled expression on his face.

"Aspirin," Eunice says patiently.

Howard touches the bump on his forehead. "Oh. Right."

"Get it with buffering added, Howard," Eunice says. "Better for your stomach."

"Right," Howard says.

19

"Front!" Fritz proclaims. He hits the bell on the desk and holds out the room keys.

"Flat." Howard walks back to the front desk. "It's flat," he says.

"Sir?" Fritz intones.

"Your bell is flat. Half a tone off." Howard smiles and walks off toward the escalator. Fritz watches him go. A bellboy takes the keys and goes with the luggage to the elevator, followed by Eunice.

Howard walks by Judy, fingering the bump on his head. She is still standing near the house phones. Judy picks up her overnight case and follows Howard to the escalators.

Mr. Smith has entered the San Francisco Bristol Hotel by the downstairs service entrance and now rides the escalator up to the main lobby. Overnight case in hand, he registers and waits patiently for Fritz to turn over his room key. He waves off a bellboy, heads for the elevator and pushes the button.

The golf bag carried by Mr. Jones has lightened considerably. There is a single club remaining in it. As he rides the escalator up to the main lobby, a young woman riding the down escalator turns to look at him strangely. Jones straightens the left lapel of his jacket, and slings the golf bag to his other shoulder. The elevator door is just closing as he gets off the escalator. He has a glimpse of Smith. Jones watches the indicator. The elevator stops at the 17th floor. Good. Jones finds a chair in the lobby and checks his watch. He puts down the golf bag. He will wait ten minutes.

Mrs. Van Hoskins and her luggage have arrived safely in room 1715. She has tipped the bellboys lightly and now begins preparations for the evening. Her overnight case is on a low bench at the foot of the bed. She rummages in the largest suitcase, extracts her low-cut sea green chiffon, then goes to the bathroom and turns the water on in the tub for her bath.

Eunice Burns is a neat woman. Five minutes after the bellboy has delivered her and the luggage to room 1714, her suit jacket and other clothes are already hung in the closet. Her wig is on its stand on the night table. Howard's overnight bag sits by Eunice's front door. She checks her watch and frowns. Howard is three minutes late. Eunice shrugs and unpacks her toilet articles, lining them up in three precise rows on the marble sink top. She takes a towel from the bathroom, places it on the bureau top, unpacks her traveling iron and lets it heat. There is a wrinkle in the dress she has brought to wear to the banquet.

Howard enters the drugstore. A tiny bell rings. It is slightly sharp. Howard shakes his head in mild disgust. At the far end of the store, by a cash register, a middle-aged balding druggist with a huge paunch stands behind a counter. The drugstore is divided into aisles by high shelves of merchandise, stacked so densely that one cannot see through to the next aisle. There are no markers. Howard moves slowly down an aisle, looking aimlessly around.

Judy enters the drugstore. The tiny bell rings. Howard turns to look at the bell. He sees a young woman carrying an overnight case and a handful of carrots. She is mildly distracting. Howard can not remember why he is in the drugstore. He moves on toward the back of the aisle. Suddenly he has the feeling that he is being watched. He stops and turns around.

Judy is looking at Howard from the front of the drugstore. Suddenly, she smiles. Confused, Howard looks behind him. There is no one else there. When he looks back, the girl is gone. He moves to another aisle, hoping he will see what it is he has come to the drugstore to buy.

Judy is peering at him around the end of the aisle.

21

He stares at her. She winks. He takes a step backward. She ducks out of sight. Howard shakes his head, wanders a few steps down the aisle and stops to look at a shelf that is stacked with souvenirs of San Francisco items and childrens' toys. Among the display items are a foot-long child's xylophone and a hunk of black rock with the legend painted on it: *The Rock— Send a Piece of Alcatraz to the Folks Back Home.*

Howard picks up the little xylophone mallet and hits a few of the metal notes. They are tinny. Then he lifts the piece of rock off the shelf, examines it and strikes it with the mallet. It produces a strange, unpleasant sound. He takes a pitchpipe out of his pocket and blows a note, hits the rock again, blows a different note, hits the rock again, then looks over at the space from which he took the rock.

Judy's face is in the space.

She is in the aisle on the other side, looking through at Howard. She is eating one of the carrot sticks that she lifted from the waiter's tray while calling room service.

Howard is poised, mallet in hand, prepared to hit the rock. He stares at Judy strangely.

Judy smiles. "What's up, Doc?"

Howard has the pitchpipe in his mouth. He puts down the mallet and removes the pitchpipe. "I beg your pardon?" he says.

Judy looks up and down the aisle. "We've got to stop meeting like this," she says.

Howard checks behind him to see if she just might be talking to someone else. There is no one there. He looks back to see if perhaps he had imagined the whole thing. The girl is still there.

"I think you're making a mistake," he says. "I'm just looking for something for . . . yes, for a headache," he remembers suddenly.

Judy looks at the rock Howard is holding. "You're going to need an awful big glass of water to get that down," she says.

"What?" Howard looks at the rock. "Oh. No. That is, you see, I'm a musicologist."

Judy looks at him blankly.

"I was just testing this specimen for inherent tonal quality," Howard explains.

"Uh-huh." Judy nods her head. Her face looks serious.

"I have this theory about early man's musical relationship to igneous rock formations," Howard explains.

"Uh-huh." Judy nods her head. She reaches through the hole in the shelf and touches the rock.

"Well," Howard says, "I guess you're not really interested in igneous rock formations."

"Not as much as I am in the metamorphic or the sedimentary rock categories," she says seriously.

Howard looks at her oddly.

"I mean," Judy continues, "I can take your igneous rocks or leave them. I relate primarily to quartz, micas, and feldspar. You can keep your pyroxenes, magnetics, and coarse-grained plutonics."

Howard looks at Judy a long, long time. "I've forgotten why I came in here," he says at last.

"Headache."

"Yes, thank you. And good-bye." Howard carefully puts the rock back in its place on the shelf, obscuring Judy's face. He pockets the pitchpipe and, still carrying the xylophone mallet, he moves down the aisle and around it to another aisle where he finally sees his shelves of drugs. He finds the pain section and bends down to find some buffered aspirin. He pulls out a large bottle to check the label.

Judy's face is in the space.

"Was it something I said?" she asks plaintively.

23

"I beg your pardon?"

"Listen," she says dramatically. "What do you think I am? A piece of ripe fruit that you can squeeze the juice out of and then cast aside?"

"Miss—I think you're making a mistake . . . ."

"Sure," she interrupts. "That's all I am to you. A mistake. A clerical error. Erase me. Forget you even know my name!"

"I *don't* know your name," Howard points out.

"Judy Maxwell." She reaches her hand through the space. Howard takes her hand and shakes it automatically.

"How do you do?" he says.

Judy does not release his hand.

"Could you let go of my hand now?" Howard asks.

"I don't think so," Judy says seriously.

Howard pulls back suddenly. Judy lets go of his hand and he falls backward, sweeping dozens of packages off the shelf as he falls. Judy rushes around the aisle to help.

"Oh, dear, look what happened."

"Please don't help me," Howard says quickly. "I'm perfectly able to do it myself."

"You've got to be more careful," Judy says seriously. "You know—three percent of all fatal accidents in the United States take place in the corner drugstore."

"Hey—what's going on back there?" the druggist calls.

"Nothing," Judy says hurriedly. "We're just looking for some aspirin."

Howard starts putting the spilled boxes back on the shelf.

"Let me help you," Judy offers.

"No, I'd rather you just went away," Howard tells her.

"Okay."

Eunice Burns is getting nervous. There is too much at stake. Howard must arrive at the banquet on time. He is often late. There is no choice. She will have to go find him. Quickly she gets back into her suit, checks to make sure the iron is turned off, adjusts her wig and, taking her room key, she locks the door of room 1714 and heads for the elevator.

Mrs. Van Hoskins has forgotten to close the tub drain. She looks in disgust at the two inches of water in the tub. She will be late. She adjusts the drain so the tub will fill and goes to hang her new clothes in the closet. There are a great many of them.

Judy Maxwell wanders about the drugstore as Howard rearranges boxes on the shelf. He remembers to set aside some buffered aspirin. Judy spots a clock radio, takes it from the shelf and brings it to the druggist at the counter. The druggist is scowling at Howard.

"My husband will pay for this," Judy tells the druggist, putting the clock radio on the counter.

"What's he doing on the floor back there?" the druggist asks.

"Please," Judy says quietly. "He suffers from a nervous condition. He falls down a lot."

"I don't want people falling down in here," the druggist tells Judy.

"Well," she explains, "we're on our honeymoon." She smiles sweetly at the druggist and moves away from the counter to browse at a rack of paperbacks.

The druggist checks the price tag on the radio and rings it up on the cash register.

Finally, Howard comes to the back of the drugstore, holding a bottle of aspirin and the mallet from the xylophone. The druggist picks up the mallet and looks at Howard questioningly. Howard shrugs.

"Is this the kind of aspirin with buffering?" Howard asks.

"That's right."

"How much do I owe you?" Howard asks.

The druggist rings up the aspirin on the cash register. "Sixty-eight twenty-nine," he says.

"I beg your pardon?" Howard says.

"Sixty-eight dollars and twenty-nine cents," the druggist repeats.

Howard looks at the bottle in his hand with a puzzled expression. "How much is it without the buffering?" he asks.

"Look mister," the druggist says patiently, "the aspirin is eighty-four cents. This is sixty-seven forty-five." He points to the radio.

"What's that?" Howard asks.

"A radio," the druggist says impatiently.

"Radio? I don't want a radio," Howard says.

"What about your wife?" the druggist asks. He looks over at Judy who smiles back innocently.

"I don't want a wife. I mean—I haven't got a wife."

"Aw, come on, Steve," Judy says to Howard. "Quit kidding around."

"I don't know who you are," Howard tells Judy. He turns back to the druggist. "I don't know who she is."

"Come on, Steve," the druggist says. "Buy her the radio. It's on sale."

Howard begins to back toward the door of the drugstore, leaving the aspirin on the druggist's counter.

Judy calls after him. "*You call this a honeymoon!*"

Howard turns and half runs for the door.

"Steve! Hey, Steve!"

Judy runs after Howard.

"Hey, what about the aspirin?" The druggist calls out after Judy.

26

The tiny bell rings.

Howard is just getting onto the up escalator when Judy catches up with him.

"Steve! Wait!"

Howard turns on the bottom step of the escalator. Judy puts out a hand and grabs his jacket. The escalator takes him up and his jacket rips along the back seam.

"Oh," Judy wails. "I'm terribly sorry."

Howard comes back down the up escalator with difficulty. He cranes his neck to look at the damage to his jacket.

"I'm terribly sorry," Judy says. "Let me sew it up for you, Steve. We can go someplace quiet. Let's go in the drugstore and get a needle and thread."

"I don't want to go back in the drugstore," Howard says. "I don't like the drugstore." His voice is surprisingly calm.

He starts toward the up escalator once again. Judy blocks his way. Howard gets onto the down escalator and begins climbing it. Judy gets on the up escalator. When they are side by side, she turns around and begins walking down. They talk as they walk.

"Now listen, Steve . . . ."

"Look here. My name isn't Steve. It's Howard Bannister. And now that I've told you that, I wish you'd forget you ever heard it."

"Okay," Judy says solemnly. "I like Steve better anyway."

Howard talks to Judy as if she were a small child. "Obviously, you've mistaken me for somebody else. Now would you just leave me alone."

"Why did you follow me into the drugstore?" Judy asks suddenly.

Howard is caught off guard. He retreats a step on the escalator and Judy walks a bit faster until they are level once again. They are nearing the top of the escalators. Howard thinks hard.

"I didn't follow you into the drugstore," he says finally. "I had a headache."

"Still have it?" Judy asks.

Howard fingers the bump on his head. He thinks a second. "No," he says.

"See?" Judy gestures in triumph.

"*Howard!*"

He looks up. Judy looks around. It is Eunice, standing at the top of the escalators. Her face is set in a fierce scowl. "I said *five* minutes," she says.

"I'm sorry, Eunice," Howard says.

"Eunice?" Judy says. "My God—that's a person named Eunice." Judy turns around to ride the remaining distance to the lobby facing in the proper direction, staring at Eunice in disbelief.

Howard walks faster. He and Judy reach the top of the escalators at the same time.

"Where *have* you been?" Eunice asks Howard, glancing quickly at Judy and then turning her back.

"I had a little problem in the drugstore," Howard explains.

"Steve," Judy interrupts, "you didn't tell me you were married!"

"We're not married," Howard says.

"Congratulations," Judy says brightly.

"But we will be soon," Eunice adds quickly.

"Condolences," Judy says.

"Who is this person?" Eunice asks Howard.

"I don't have the vaguest idea," he says. "She was behind a rock in the drugstore."

"Aw, come on, Steve." Judy pokes him in the leg with her overnight case. "You can tell her about me."

Eunice's nervous twitch begins to appear over an eye. Her hands are clenching and unclenching.

"Why is she calling you by that name?" Eunice asks Howard in a shrill voice.

Howard tries to pull Eunice away. "Don't pay any attention to her." He pleads with Judy, "Look, Miss Maxwell . . . ."

"You know her name!" Eunice shrieks.

"Eunice—I swear—it's—it's some kind of bizarre joke," Howard says desperately.

Judy backs toward the down escalator. "Sure," she says. "It's easy for you! Everywhere you go, another heart broken. Women, women, women! You call it *joking*. But Eunice and I call it—*lust*."

To Howard's horror and Eunice's consternation, people in the lobby have begun to stop and listen. A man wearing a brown suit, a golfbag at his side, is staring frankly.

Eunice says to Judy with righteous indignation, "Don't you know the meaning of *propriety?*"

Judy steps onto the escalator and begins to go down, disappearing. "Propriety," she says. "Noun; conformity to established standards of behavior or manners; suitability; rightness or justness. See 'etiquette'. . . ."

Judy is gone from sight.

Howard and Eunice, who is twitching badly, stand still and look at the now empty escalator.

vor. Howard's overnight case is on top of the
bureau. Bettina is having some trouble arranging
thoughts of the printouts with Judy's pictures.

Room 1712, connected to Eunice's room, is . . .

CHAPTER THREE

In the San Francisco Bristol, one finds an even-
numbered room to the left of the elevators. Odd-num-
bered rooms are to the right. The seventeenth floor is
no exception.

Room 1711, unoccupied at present, connects with
room 1713, in which Mr. Smith is pacing the floor. His
overnight case sits on the bureau. The door connecting
his room to 1715 is securely locked. It was one of the
first things he had checked. Smith is feeling nervous.
He wonders why he has stopped smoking.

In room 1715, Mrs. Van Hoskins is almost ready for
her bath. She checks the water. It is way too hot. In
disgust she lets out half the water, restops the drain,
and adjusts the spigots more to her liking. Her overnight case is still on the bench at the foot of the bed.

Room 1717, to the right of Mrs. Van Hoskins', is
presently vacant.

Directly across the hall from 1717, in room 1716,
Howard Bannister is dressing for the banquet. The
bump on his forehead no longer hurts, but it is a bit
noticeable. He is having some trouble discarding
thoughts of Judy Maxwell.

One room closer to the elevators, in 1714, which
connects with Howard's, Eunice Burns is setting her

wig. Howard's overnight case is now on one of the twin beds. Eunice is having some trouble discarding thoughts of the encounter with Judy Maxwell.

Room 1712, connecting to Eunice's room, is unoccupied, and connects with room 1710, now being left by the musicologist, Hugh Simon. Dressed informally, Simon enters the elevator he has summoned, descends to the main floor, crosses the lobby and heads for the Bristol's banquet room.

Two elevators service the seventeenth floor. The indicator on the one to the left has just passed fourteen. It is the one to the right that has been used by Hugh Simon. As Simon nears the banquet's receptionists, the elevator is claimed by Mr. Jones, carrying his golf bag.

The left elevator bell rings; the door to the 17th floor corridor opens and a waiter steps out. He is carrying a tray covered with a white cloth. He checks the numbers to his right, stops and places the tray quietly before the door of room 1717. As he does so, the right elevator bell rings; the door opens and Jones, carrying his golf bag with the one club, steps out. Jones walks slowly down the hall, looking at the doors to his left as if checking for his room. He nods at the waiter.

"Good evening, sir," the waiter whispers.

"Good evening," Jones whispers back.

"Don't want to wake the little one," the waiter explains.

"No. Sure don't," Jones whispers back.

The waiter returns down the hall and into an elevator. The door closes. Jones immediately walks back to the elevators and starts working his way down the corridor. He gets down on his hands and knees to listen and peer under each door.

In room 1715, there is the sound of water running. And on a low bench at the foot of the bed, there is an

31

overnight case. Jones smiles and leans back on his heels, satisfied.

Judy Maxwell sticks the little package into her overnight case. She has talked the druggist into charging her purchase to room 1717. The carrots are gone, and it is definitely dinner time. After she eats, she will check at the desk for the room number she needs. Judy walks up the up escalator, crosses the lobby and gets into an elevator.

Harry, the house dick, checks his watch, then looks over at Fritz. They nod to each other. Harry folds his newspaper carefully, places it in a magazine rack near his chair, and heads for the elevators.

Jones, who had been lying on the floor in front of the door to room 1715, stands suddenly and retrieves his golf bag. There is the sound of a door opening. It is Howard, who walks into the hall from room 1716. He is dressed for the banquet, except for a plaid bow tie which he holds in his hand.

Jones moves quickly in front of room 1717 and tries to look nonchalant. There is a slight look of terror in Jones' eye. Howard smiles at him.

"Just looking for my key," Jones whispers.

"Oh—yes," Howard whispers back. He moves to room 1714, leaving his door slightly ajar.

Jones unslings the golf bag from his shoulder and leans it quietly against the door of room 1717, stepping around the tray on the floor. Howard lifts his hand to knock on Eunice's door. He looks back at Jones, who is still pretending to search for a key.

"Can't seem to find it," Jones whispers.

"Maybe the door is open," Howard whispers back.

"No, no," Jones whispers, shaking his head. "I'm sure I locked it." But because Howard is watching, Jones tries the door handle. Much to his horror, the handle turns and the weight of the golf bag leaning on the door causes it to swing open. Jones looks into the room, fearing the worst.

To his great relief and surprise, room 1717 is obviously unoccupied. Jones steps boldly into the room and looks back at Howard. "Good night," he whispers.

"Don't forget your dinner," Howard whispers back.

"Yes. I'll get it later. Thanks," Jones whispers. He closes the door to room 1717 behind him.

Howard knocks softly on the door to room 1714. "Eunice. Eunice," he whispers.

"Who's there?"

"It's me," Howard whispers. "Howard Bannister. Your fiancé."

The door opens. Eunice is wearing a blue quilted bathrobe with white daisies. Her face is bare of make-up. She eyes Howard with approval. "Ah," she says. "You look very nice, Howard."

"Thank you," he whispers. "You look very nice, too, Eunice."

"I haven't gotten dressed yet, Howard," Eunice says patiently.

"I wondered about that," Howard whispers.

"Why are you whispering, Howard?" Eunice asks.

"I—I'm not at all sure," he whispers.

"Well, *stop it.*"

"I will," he whispers. "I mean," Howard continues in a normal voice, "I will."

Eunice stands away from the door. "Well, come in. I'll do your tie."

"What tie is that, Eunice?" Howard asks.

"*Your tie. The tie in your hand.*" Eunice grabs the bow tie in exasperation.

"Oh yes, of course," Howard says.

He comes into the room. As Howard closes the door behind him, the elevator at the end of the corridor opens and Judy Maxwell steps out, carrying her overnight case. She walks down the hall to room 1717, checks the number on the door and then bends down and lifts the napkin covering the tray on the floor. It is her roast beef sandwich. She licks her lips and wonders briefly how to manage the tray and her overnight case.

The elevator bell rings.

Judy looks down the hall. The elevator door is opening. She looks around quickly, notices that the door to room 1716 is ajar, and with a fond parting look at her sandwich, she crosses the hall and enters room 1716, closing the door behind her.

It is Harry who steps out of the elevator into the corridor. He walks down the hall, stops in front of room 1715, gets on his hands and knees and peers under the door. On the bench before the bed he can see Mrs. Van Hoskins' overnight case. There is the sound of a door being opened. Harry stands up quickly.

The door to room 1717 opens and Jones looks out. Jones and Harry stare at each other for a moment, smiling nervously. Jones points to the tray on the floor. "Ah—my dinner is here," he says.

Harry walks down the hall to room 1711, takes out a passkey, opens the door and goes inside. Jones has picked up the tray and is backing into room 1717.

The door to room 1716 opens and Judy steps out. She looks at Jones, and at the tray with her roast beef sandwich that he is holding. Jones smiles at her nervously. "Ahh—my dinner," he says, and steps back inside the room with the tray, shutting the door.

"I don't know who he is but I hate him," Judy mutters to herself. She goes back inside room 1716 and shuts the door. She stands leaning against it, wondering what to do next. Her overnight case is on the floor. She picks it up, crosses the room and puts it on the bureau. On the bureau is Howard's torn jacket and his room key. Judy picks up the jacket and looks at it, examining the torn seam. A smile of pleasure lights up her face. Judy opens her overnight case and extracts the package from the drugstore.

Howard is standing in front of the mirror in room 1714. Eunice is standing behind him, tying his bow tie. Howard's igneous rock formations, in his overnight case, are on one of the twin beds.

"Howard," Eunice is saying, "you must have said something to encourage that girl."

"Like what?" Howard asks.

"Well, Howard," Eunice says patiently, "I think you know what I'm talking about. After all, you are a *man*."

Howard nods his head. "Yes. Right That's absolutely right."

"And she is a *woman*," Eunice continues.

"Right again," Howard agrees.

"In the same way that *I* am a woman," Eunice says patiently. "Do you see what I mean?"

Howard turns around. "Eunice! I don't think of you that way. I don't think of you as a woman. I mean—I think of you as—as—*Eunice*."

"But I *am* a woman, Howard."

"Oh. Of course. I know *that*."

"Then you *do* think of me as a woman," Eunice prods.

"Yes. In a way," Howard concedes.

"In a way?"

"Let me put it this way, Eunice," Howard explains. "At no time have I ever thought of you as, say, a man."

"I see." With a flourish Eunice finishes tying Howard's bow tie.

"Eunice—I know that I don't seem to be a very—ah —romantic person, but . . . ."

35

"I'm not looking for romance, Howard," Eunice interrupts.

"Oh," Howard says with relief.

"I'm looking for something more important than that, something stronger," Eunice explains. "As the years go by, romance fades and something else takes its place. Do you know what that is?"

Howard thinks hard. "Senility?" he offers.

"Trust," Eunice says.

"That's what I meant," Howard quickly agrees.

"I think we'd better talk about this some other time," Eunice says briskly, checking her watch. "I don't want you to be late for the banquet. I'll be down in a few minutes. Now, Howard—I want you to make a good impression on Mr. Larrabee. I want you to tell me exactly what you're going to say to him."

"Well," Howard says, "I'll probably say something like—uh—'Hello there, Mr. Larrabee. I'm Howard.' "

Eunice throws a hand up to her forehead, where the tic once again threatens. "You are not!" she exclaims.

"I'm not *Howard?*" Howards asks, confused.

"You are *not* going to say, 'Hi, my name is Howard.' Anyone can say that. *Anyone.*"

"Anyone named Howard," Howard says.

Eunice ignores this. "You are going to walk straight up to him," she instructs, "take his hand in a firm masculine handshake and say, 'Mr. Larrabee, I am Dr. Howard Bannister.' Do you think you can do that?"

"I think so," Howard says, repeating the line to himself.

Eunice leads Howard to the door. "Well, do your best," she tells him. "Be dignified."

"I'll be dignified." Howard turns the door handle and tries to push the door open.

"Be solemn, but not stuffy," Eunice is saying.

36

Howard is pushing at the door. "I'll be solemn," he repeats.

"Act friendly, but impersonal."

Howard works at opening the door. "I'll be friendly," he says.

"*Pull* the door open," Eunice says.

"I'll pull the door open."

Howard pulls the door open and with great relief steps out into the corridor. Eunice comes to the door of her room.

"Well, good-bye, Eunice."

"Now, don't be nervous, Howard." Eunice reaches up and gives his bow tie a last-minute straightening. "Just remember, everything depends on this."

Howard walks toward the elevators. Eunice closes the door of room 1714 behind her.

Howard mumbles to himself as he walks. "Now— Mr. Larrabee, it's a . . . it's an honor . . . no, it's a. . . ." He stops in front of room 1711, trying to remember the speech.

The door to room 1711 opens, and Harry, the house dick, starts out.

Howard has remembered his speech. "It's a privilege to meet you," he says.

Harry stares at Howard, completely confused. "Likewise," Harry says. He steps back in the room and closes the door as Howard goes to the elevator and pushes the button.

Judy is sitting on the bed in room 1716. She is sewing up the torn seam in Howard's jacket with the needle and thread she charged in the drugstore. She finishes, bites the thread off, puts the needle into her case, which sits on the bed next to her, its top open. She stands and holds the jacket up, looking at it, then crosses with it to the closet. As she passes the bureau, she stops to pick up an envelope she had not noticed

37

before. In elegant, handwritten script, it says: *Larrabee Foundation Banquet Invitation.*

Judy's stomach growls. She lowers the invitation, pats it thoughtfully at her chin, and smiles at her reflection in the mirror.

CHAPTER FOUR

In the ballroom of the hotel, there is a queue around the splendid cold hors d'oeuvres table which is set against a wall beneath a large banner that reads *Congress of American Musicologists*. Dual centerpieces, elaborate displays of white roses, black olives, radishes, candied violets and grapes are in the form of the treble and bass clef symbols. Tables for eight are set in a large semicircle before the rectangular main table, and throughout the banquet room small groups of guests stand in animated conversation. Crabmeat tidbits, cheese puffs and other hot hors d'oeuvres are carried on trays by circulating waiters. The musicologists have dressed for the occasion. The men are in formal wear; the women are gowned. The champagne flows; old acquaintances are being renewed.

Howard stops at the desk outside the banquet hall and collects his name tag from the receptionist. The card is handwritten, enclosed in plastic; the pin is attached to the back. Howard enters the room, fumbles with his card and finally gets it pinned on. A formally dressed man is approaching. Howard smiles and holds out his hand.

"Mr. Larrabee," Howard says warmly, "it's a priviledge to meet you. I'm Dr. Howard Bannister."

39

"And I am your headwaiter, Rudy. Can I show you to your table, sir?" Rudy asks.

"Oh, no, thank you," Howard says, still offering a handshake. "I think I'll just sort of mingle for a while."

Rudy takes a glass from the tray of a passing waiter and puts it into Howard's hand. "Here you are, sir," Rudy says.

"Oh, thank you. I don't drink," Howard says.

Rudy looks at Howard's name tag, which he has pinned on upside down.

"You're upside down, sir," Rudy tells him.

Howard looks totally confused as he watches Rudy move off and across the banquet room. "I'm upside down," he says to himself.

Judy Maxwell, in room 1716, has emptied the contents of her overnight case on the bed. It contains a surprising number of wrinkle-free clothes, cosmetics, a three-volume desk encyclopedia, a pair of gold-heeled bedroom mules, which she decides will do, and a white silk pants suit. It had been a splurge and, as she lifts it up, a pleased smile crosses her face. Judy dresses quickly, changes her earrings and puts the room key in her little purse. She repacks her overnight case, and decides to leave it in the bathroom, under the sink. She is ready. She gives herself a last minute look in the mirror, blots her lipstick, leaves the room and heads for the elevator, carrying the banquet invitation.

In room 1715, Mrs. Van Hoskins has finally finished her bath and, dressed in an impressively scanty lingerie set, she sits at the night table applying make-up. Her overnight case is now open on the dresser, and several pieces of jewelry—a diamond and emerald brooch, two diamond bracelets, a gold rope necklace and a pair of gold and diamond earrings—are lying beside it. She will surely change her mind.

40

In room 1714, Eunice Burns is working on her wig. She is not happy. The ends of the flip are flopping. She decides to give it one last try with the curlers. It cannot be helped. Her evening clothes are laid out neatly on the bed, next to Howard's overnight case.

In room 1717, Mr. Jones has thoroughly enjoyed the roast beef sandwich. He had not realized how hungry he was and he says a silent thanks to his unknown benefactor. His golf bag lies on one of the twin beds and now, finished eating, he walks silently to the door connecting with room 1715, and puts his ear to it. There are noises he can not identify. He wonders what Smith is doing.

In room 1711, Harry checks his watch. Mrs. Van Hoskins is going to be very late. She is always very late. He lies down on a bed and watches the ceiling. He will give her fifteen minutes.

Howard is standing alone in the center of the banquet room, the glass of champagne in his hand. He has been holding it for many minutes. He takes an hors d'oeuvre from the tray offered by a uniformed waitress and as a waiter with a tray of empty glasses walks past, Howard makes a great effort and finally gets rid of his glass. He turns to look at the door, wondering what is detaining Eunice, and as he does so, a fresh glass of champagne is thrust into his hand.

From the crowd around the buffet table, a large, shaggy-haired man heads toward Howard. He is wearing a sport jacket and a red and white striped tie. He is carrying a glass of champagne.

He stops near Howard, cocks his head to one side and momentarily sizes him up before walking closer.

"I am Hugh Simon," he says to Howard. He speaks with a slight, unidentifiable, middle-European accent.

"How do you do?" Howard says. He holds out his

hand. Simon ignores it and peers over his glasses at Howard's name tag.

"You're upside down," Simon points out.

"I know," Howard says.

Simon cocks his head and reads the tag. "So," he says. "*You* are Howard Ballister."

"Bannister," Howard says.

"*I* am Hugh Simon," Simon says, waiting for Howard to react.

"That's nice," Howard says. He finally lowers his hand.

Simon sips his champagne and contemplates Howard over the rim of his glass. "I suppose you haven't read my series of articles in *Music Monthly* on the 'Versuch einer Anweisung,'" Simon says finally.

"I haven't," Howard acknowledges. "I'm terribly sorry."

"Foolish of you," Simon says. "You must realize that those articles helped me to become one of the two finalists in contention for the Larrabee grant." He steps back to look at Howard again. "Amazingly," he says, shaking his head in disbelief, "you are the other one."

"Oh," Howard says.

"I can't imagine that the Larrabee Foundation will throw good money away on a study of prehistoric rock thumpings." Simon reaches out and spears several cheese puffs from the tray of a passing waiter.

"Well," Howard says pleasantly, "actually, I think you're over simplifying my thesis. You see . . . ."

"*Over simplifying!*" Simon interrupts. "You accuse me of over simplifying! I *never* over simplify." Simon raises himself on his heels. "There's an old Croatian saying, Bollixter, which goes. . . ."

There has been a sudden, dramatic increase in the noise level in the banquet room. Simon interrupts himself and looks around. The banquet guests have turned in the direction of the door. A man in his thirties, short, his hair long, wearing fashionable evening clothes with a large black bow tie, is entering the room.

"Ahh," Simon says. "At last. Our host."

"Mr. Larrabee?" Howard asks.

Simon ignores him.

A number of the guests move toward Larrabee as he enters the room. Some of them applaud. Larrabee acknowledges the applause with a slight nod, and begins working his way around the room, shaking hands, nodding and greeting friends.

Simon thrusts his champagne glass into Howard's empty hand, leaving himself free to applaud wildly. Howard ponders the two glasses, makes a feeble attempt to join the clapping, but discovers immediately that with a glass in each hand it is impossible. He looks around anxiously for a solution to his problem.

Larrabee has half crossed the length of the banquet room, and as he gets nearer and nearer to Simon and Howard, Simon's applause gets more enthusiastic.

Larrabee comes to a stop a few feet away. He looks at the glasses in Howard's hands, smiles and nods, and then nods to Simon who is now the only person in the room still applauding. Simon continues to clap. Larrabee continues to nod. Slowly, Simon stops clapping and Larrabee stops nodding. Larrabee looks relieved.

Howard takes a deep breath. "Mr. Larrabee," he says, "it's a . . . ."

Simon steps between Howard and Mr. Larrabee. He grasps Larrabee's hand and pumps it avidly, turning Larrabee around so that his back is toward Howard.

"I'm Hugh Simon, Mr. Larrabee," he says. "I'd like to say—oh, I love your hair!" He continues without a pause. "On behalf of myself and all of my colleagues at the Conservatory . . . ."

"Yes, indeed," Mr. Larrabee interrupts. "Yes, in-

43

deed." He removes his hand from Simon's and turns around to Howard. "I believe this must be . . . ."

Howard says, "It's a great, uh . . . ."

Simon deftly turns Larrabee back away from Howard. Once again he pumps Larrabee's hand. "Mr. Larrabee," Simon says, "although I want you to know that I, personally, have nothing but contempt for monetary gain, the twenty thousand dollars will allow us—*me*, that is—to bring to a successful conclusion a body of work that will most certainly reflect *une gloire enorme* on the Larrabee Foundation."

Larrabee retrieves his hand from Simon's. "Yes, yes, yes. Very well put, Mr. Simon," Larrabee says. "Nothing like a little *gloire, enorme* or otherwise. But I must point out that you are only one of the finalists and, if I'm not mistaken, this is the other." Larrabee moves back a step to escape Simon, and finally manages to turn back toward Howard.

"It's a Larrabee," Howard says.

Simon once again corners Larrabee, turning him away from Howard. "Believe me, I understand Mr. Larrabee . . . ."

"Very understanding of you, Simon," Larrabee says firmly. "Very understanding. And now, if you don't mind."

Larrabee pulls suddenly and with determination away from Simon and turns abruptly back toward Howard, who has moved directly behind him. They collide, and the champagne in the glass Simon had put into Howard's hand spills.

"Oh," Howard says. "I'm . . . terribly sorry." He steps back and tries to keep the champagne from dripping on himself and Larrabee. Howard looks down at his feet and does a little dance to avoid the liquid. When he stops, finally, Howard looks up to see Larrabee watching him.

Larrabee smiles in greeting and cocks his head slightly to read Howard's upside-down name tag.

Howard, with a slight smile, cocks his head to return the greeting, and gathers his breath to finally introduce himself.

Larrabee straightens up and extends his hand. "Bannister," he says.

"Ahh," Howard says happily. "Uh—Mr. Privilege, it's a Larrabee to. . . ." Howard stops in confusion. "No, it isn't that. It isn't that at all. Well, I'm sure glad to see you," he manages finally. Howard extends a hand with a glass in it to shake hands.

"Thank you," Larrabee says. "I don't drink."

"Neither do I," Howard says.

Larrabee looks at the glasses in Howard's hands. "You don't?" he says. "Then—shall we sit down, gentlemen? I believe we're all sharing the main table."

"After you, sir," Simon says, quickly coming to Larrabee's side. Howard falls in behind.

In room 1715, Mrs. Van Hoskins is finally dressed for the evening in her green chiffon. She has now dumped all of her jewelry on the dresser top and stands before the mirror, making a decision. In the end, she wears the heavy gold necklace, the diamond and emerald brooch, a bracelet, two of her rings, and a simple pair of three-carat pear-shaped diamond earrings. She tosses the rest of her extensive jewelry collection back in her overnight case, closes and locks it, and leaves it on the bureau top. She is half-an-hour late. William Lockland III will be waiting in the lobby. Mrs. Van Hoskins puts her room key in her purse, locks the door behind her and heads for the elevator.

Across the hall, in room 1714, Eunice Burns is working on her wig. She has left her electric rollers in a minute too long, and the nervous tic above her eye is once again threatening. She is dressed in her stockings and shoes, bra, girdle, and a full slip. She closes her eyes and with an application of willpower, she commands the tic to go away.

In room 1713, Mr. Smith is pacing the floor. The overnight case containing the documents sits on the bed. Suddenly, on impulse, he unlocks the case and opens it. The folders are there, just as they were in the airport terminal. He closes the case and places it on the bureau. He checks his watch. He wishes he had brought a sandwich and something to read.

In room 1711, Harry has fallen asleep. It had not been his intention to do so. Nor is it a serious mistake. After long years of forced sitting in hotel-lobby easy chairs, he has developed the habit of catnapping. He will awaken in ten minutes and probably wonder for a second why there is no newspaper in his hands.

In room 1717, Jones' adrenalin has started to flow. The door to the hall corridor from room 1715 has opened and closed. Jones scurries to the front door of his room, and listens for the elevator bell to ring, and for its door to open and close. He then quickly returns to the connecting door. He takes a cellophane strip from his pocket and with it he carefully forces the latch. He enters room 1715. Mrs. Van Hoskins' overnight case is on the bureau top. He quickly crosses the room, picks up the case, and takes it back into room 1717, closing the door behind him and making sure it is relocked. He tries the lid of the overnight case; it does not open. He shrugs. He will let someone else worry about that.

Jones puts the case on the bed next to his golf bag, and lifts the room phone, seating himself on the edge of the chair. He gives the operator a number.

"Give me the Chief," he says quietly into the phone. "Oh—he is?" Jones thinks a minute. "Well," he says, "okay. Tell him—*I've got the documents.*" Jones hangs up and settles back into the chair, looking at the case on the bed with affectionate satisfaction.

The Chief will be very pleased.

In the banquet room, Larrabee has come to Howard's aid, summoning a passing waiter who takes the two empty glasses away on his tray. The small groups of musicologists are breaking up as the guests go to find their seats at the tables. As Larrabee, Howard and Simon approach the main table, a tall thin man, red-faced and smiling, breaks away from the crowd at the main table and comes to greet Larrabee. He leaves behind a group of men standing and listening attentively to someone already seated at the table.

"Good evening, Professor Hosquith," Larrabee says. "Allow me to introduce you. This is Howard Bannister and Hugh . . . ."

"Ah, you're Bannister," Professor Hosquith interrupts. His voice identifies him as a Texan. "Your fiancee was just telling us about your most incredible adventure in the sky." Hosquith gestures in the direction of the group of men standing around the main table. Hosquith takes Howard's hand and pumps it vigorously. Simon looks visibly upset.

"What's this, Hosquith? Bannister, what incredible adventure did you have?" Larrabee asks.

"Yes, Howard, do tell," Simon says nastily.

"What adventure did I *have?*" Howard says to Larrabee. He turns to Professor Hosquith. "What adventure *did* I have?" Howard asks.

Hosquith shakes a finger at Howard as if it were a metronome. "Ah, you mustn't be modest about a thing like that, Bannister," Hosquith admonishes. "Simply incredible," he says to Larrabee.

Another of the men breaks away from the group around the person at the main table. He walks to

47

Howard, hand outstretched, Howard shakes hands automatically. "Good show, Bannister! Good show!" the man says.

Howard nods his head dumbly.

Simon turns his head to the ceiling and exhales noisily through tightly-clenched teeth.

Howard is staring without comprehension at Hosquith and the other man who has congratulated him, and then he turns to look at the table where the men have moved aside enough for him to see that they are gathered around Judy Maxwell. She is sitting near the head of the table, a complacent smile on her face.

Howard involuntarily begins to move toward the table, his mouth open in protest, but Larrabee beats him to it.

"And this must be Miss Burns," Larrabee says. He leans to read Judy's name tag. It says: *Eunice Burns*.

Howard moves around Larrabee and leans over to read Judy's name tag. Larrabee is shaking Judy's hand; she is smiling at Larrabee warmly. The other men around the table look as if they have been hanging on her every word. Judy turns her engaging smile to Howard.

Howard has double-checked. He can not believe it. The name tag on this person reads *Eunice Burns*, but the person is Judy Maxwell. He rubs his eyes. She is still there.

"*You!* You—you . . ." Howard says finally. He points at Judy in growing horror.

". . . nice. Eu-*nice*, Howard. Eunice," Judy says. "We've almost got that stammer cured," she explains to Larrabee. "Sit down, dear," Judy says to Howard.

Howard is paralyzed. "How—how . . . ."

"How-*ard*," Judy says, as if to a child. "Howard." She turns to Larrabee apologetically. "He still gets stuck on names," she explains. "Probably the excitement of meeting you for the first time. I must admit, I can feel it myself." Judy smiles at Larrabee, asking for his understanding, and bats her eyelashes.

"Can you?" Larrabee asks.

"*Can I?* My heart is going a mile a minute," she says. "Why, you can just feel it pounding." Judy takes Larrabee's hand, which she is still holding, and applies it near her heart.

"Can't you feel it?" she asks sweetly.

Larrabee is definitely affected. "Yes," he says. "Yes, I think—*yes*, I *can*. Absolutely. It's certainly in there —pounding. Amazing." Larrabee turns to the other men around the table. "You should feel it, gentlemen," he says seriously.

Several of the men rise from their seats.

Larrabee gains control of himself. "*Sit down*, please, gentlemen. Please." Larrabee removes his hand from Judy's dress and smiles at her. "May I sit next to you, Miss Burns?" he asks.

"I wouldn't have it any other way," Judy assures him.

Larrabee, obviously pleased, sits next to Judy. "Why don't you sit here on my right, Bannister?" Larrabee says to Howard. "Would you move, Mr. Simon, please?"

Simon, who was about to grab the seat on that side of Larrabee, paces behind the table angrily, snarling to himself in frustration.

"But, Mr. Larrabee," Howard says, "this is not— this is definitely not . . . ."

"I know, Bannister," Larrabee interrupts. "This is not the seating arrangement, according to the place cards. But I think we can break a few of the minor social customs." He smiles at Howard, and turns to beam at Judy. Judy pats Larrabee on the hand.

"Sit down, Howard," she says sweetly.

"But, sir," Howard says. "I must point out to you . . . ."

"Bannister," Larrabee interrupts firmly. "*I* must point out that a foolish consistency is the hobgoblin of little minds."

"Emerson," Judy says.

"I beg your pardon, my dear?" Larrabee says.

"Ralph Waldo Emerson. Born 1803, died 1882." Judy's recitation is given in a precise voice.

"You like Emerson?" Larrabee asks.

"I adore him," Judy says.

Howard, still stunned, finally moves to the chair on the other side of Larrabee and sits down.

"I adore anyone who adores Emerson," Larrabee is telling Judy.

"And I adore anyone who adores anyone who adores Emerson," Judy gushes. She grins. "Your turn," she says.

Larrabee chuckles with pleasure, and turns to Howard. "She's a delight, Bannister. A delight. And you're a lucky dog." He pokes Howard in the ribs. "Aren't you? Admit it. Admit you're a lucky dog," Larrabee prods.

"I'm a lucky dog," Howard says faintly. "But sir. . . ."

Larrabee is not listening. He has returned his attention to Judy. "Miss Burns, may I call you—Eunice?" he asks.

"No!" Howard says loudly.

"How's that?" Larrabee asks, turning back to Howard.

Judy explains quickly, "What Howard means is that back where we come from, everyone calls me 'Burnsy,' " she says.

"Burnsy? Burnsy." Larrabee rolls it around on his

50

tongue, trying it out. "I like that," he says finally. *"Burnsy."*

"Help," Howard says quietly to himself.

On the 17th floor, Eunice is finally under control. Her auburn wig is neatly flipped up at the ends, her gown is wrinkle-free, her tic is calmed. She takes a last look in the mirror, puts her key into her purse, puts Howard's overnight case on the floor between the twin beds, closes and locks the door to room 1714, and heads down the hall to the elevator.

In room 1711, the sound of the elevator bell and its door opening and shutting has awakened Harry from his catnap. It is dark in the room, and he wonders momentarily why the lights are out in the lobby, and why he is lying down, and where his newspaper has gone. He remembers about Mrs. Van Hoskins' overnight case and the jewelry then, turns on the light, checks his watch, goes to the bathroom and washes his face with cold water.

Simon is very unhappy at being outmaneuvered. He has been pacing behind the table to regain his self-control. The other banquet guests are nearly seated now. He takes a deep breath, clenches and unclenches his fists, curses to himself in Croatian, and heads for the empty seat next to Judy at the main table.

As Simon pulls out the chair beside her, Judy looks up with her usual smile. Simon gives her his usual dyspeptic expression. Judy's smile evaporates.

"Oh-oh," she says to herself.

Larrabee plays the host that he is, and makes the introduction. "Miss Burns, this is Mr. Hugh Simon, your fiance's competitor for the Larrabee grant," Larrabee says graciously.

"The grant?" Judy says.

51

"For the twenty thousand dollars," Larrabee says with a smile, looking at Simon and Howard.

Simon's eyes brighten at the mention of the money.

"Twenty thousand—dollars?" Judy says.

"Yes," Larrabee says, "didn't you . . . ."

"Oh—of course," Judy interrupts. "The twenty thousand dollars. I just forgot about *that*."

"You forgot?" Simon asks incredulously.

"Well," Judy explains, "it seems to me that the money is secondary." She turns to smile sweetly at Larrabee. "I mean, when you consider the sheer honor of winning the Larrabee Award itself." Judy adjusts the sleeves of her jacket demurely and looks down modestly.

Larrabee beams. "Very nicely put, Miss Burns," he says. "How long have you held this theory?"

"Oh," Judy says, thinking fast. "About ten seconds," she replies truthfully.

Larrabee laughs delightedly again, to Simon's obvious fury.

Larrabee turns to Howard. "I don't think you appreciate what you've got here, Bannister, my boy," he says, slapping Howard on the back.

Howard giggles hysterically. Larrabee giggles with him. Simon turns his head away in disgust. Larrabee stops giggling suddenly, as if remembering who he is and turns back to Judy. She leans her elbows on either side of her table setting and cups her chin in her hands, leaning on Larrabee's every word.

"But seriously, Miss Burns," Larrabee says, seriously, "I know that it's a cliche, but I think you'll agree that money can't buy happiness."

"No," Judy agrees. "But it certainly can rent it for a while."

Larrabee laughs uproariously. "By gum, I like you, Miss Burns," he says.

CHAPTER FIVE

Mrs. Van Hoskins and her escort, William Lockland III, a long-time acquaintance and, in fact, the son of a college friend of her late husband's, are riding in the back seat of Mr. Lockland II's Rolls Royce. Henry, the night chauffeur, is at the wheel. As usual, they will spend the evening visiting friends, partying, and riding around San Francisco.

Mrs. Van Hoskins visits San Francisco for a week, six times a year and it is with great pleasure that William Lockland III anticipates each visit. Not only does his father fork over the Rolls—Mrs. Van Hoskins likes to be driven, but she is very generous.

Lockland leans toward the driver. "The restaurant now, Henry," he says. He turns and smiles warmly at Mrs. Van Hoskins, and taking her hand, he tucks it firmly under his arm.

In room 1713 of the San Francisco Bristol, Mr. Smith makes preparations to leave. He takes a last look around the room, pockets his key and, overnight case securely in hand, he opens his door a crack and peers out into the corridor. It is empty. He turns off the light and starts to walk out into the hall.

There is the sound of a door opening. It is further down the corridor. Smith quickly moves back into his room and adjusts the door so it is open merely a crack. Cautiously, he peers into the corridor.

Jones is ready. He checks the room to make sure he has not forgotten anything, adjusts the lock so he can reenter the room, if necessary, and carrying his golf bag he walks out into the corridor, leaving the overnight case inside the door as a precaution.

Smith silently shuts the door to room 1713 behind him as Jones steps into the corridor outside room 1717.

Jones is satisfied. The corridor is empty. He reaches into the room, picks up Mrs. Van Hoskins' overnight case, and starts out of the room. He hears the sound of a door, and stops.

The door to room 1711 opens and Harry, the house dick, walks out into the corridor. Harry and Mr. Jones eye each other nervously. Jones smiles and quickly turns around to make it appear that he is entering room 1717. He steps inside the room and shuts the door behind him.

Harry stands in the corridor, wondering what is going on.

In room 1713, Smith is frantically searching for a place to hide his document-filled overnight case. He looks out the window, tries to open it, but it will not budge. Finally, he goes to the door connecting his room with room 1715, and speculates for a moment. Yes. That would do, he decides. He takes a small, powerful magnet out of his pocket, places it against the lock on the door, and swivels it. The lock clicks open.

In room 1717, Jones is standing just inside the door, wondering what to do. He decides that caution is definitely indicated. There is no rush. He locks the door to his room, removes his jacket and, with Mrs.

Van Hoskins' overnight case besides him, Jones lies down on one of the twin beds to take a nap.

Harry returns to room 1711. There is no need to be hasty. Mrs. Van Hoskins will be out for several hours. There is plenty of time. He decides to wait another fifteen minutes before entering her room and taking the jewelry.

In room 1713, Smith has succeeded in opening the door connecting his room with Mrs. Van Hoskins'. He steps into the room, his overnight case in hand. He looks around the room quickly, then moves to the closet, opens the door and hides his case of documents underneath the extra hotel blankets on a top shelf. Smith closes the closet door, goes back to his room and relocks the connecting door. He feels relieved. He is also hungry. He decides on a sandwich in the coffee shop.

Harry is pacing the floor in room 1711. He has decided that a wait is foolish. With determination, he takes his passkeys from his pocket, selects the proper one for room 1715, and steps boldly into the corridor. It is empty. Harry walks quickly and stealthily to Mrs. Van Hoskins' door, opens it and enters the room. He closes the door behind him and leans against it for a moment, looking around the room for the overnight case.

Smith opens the door to the corridor and peers out. It is empty. He steps into the corridor, closes his door quietly, and goes to the elevators. He presses the button, steps into the elevator quickly when it arrives, and pushes the button for the main floor.

In the banquet room, Hugh Simon is talking with Judy. "I presume that you are familiar with your fiance's studies, Miss Burns?" Simon is saying.

"You presume correctly, Mr. Simon," Judy says.

"You've read his thesis?" Simon asks.

"I typed it for him myself," Judy says proudly.

"This is not Eunice Burns," Howard says quietly. No one is listening to him.

"Then you must share his inordinate interest in—rocks," Simon says with a slight grimace of distaste.

"Passionately," Judy says firmly. "You might even say that it was a rock that brought us together," Judy tells Simon. She leans forward to peer around Larrabee and give Howard a melting smile.

Howard tries to smile back. "You're not Eunice," he says under his breath.

"You really expect me to accept the notion that Neanderthal Man found a method of making music out of minerals?" Simon asks disdainfully of Howard, leaning forward to peer around Judy and Larrabee, who is eating his jellied consomme with pleasure.

"I believe I can prove that actual melodies—crude, of course . . . ."

"Of course," Judy agrees.

". . . but melodies, nevertheless," Howard continues, ignoring Judy, "based on the diatonic scale similar to the Norse *Ventengum* chants . . . ."

"*Love* those old Ventengums, don't you?" Judy asks Larrabee.

". . . really existed as far back as seven million B.C.," Howard says, staring at Judy with complete disapproval.

"You can prove this?" Simon asks contemptuously.

"Well—given the time—and the—uh—money, of course," Howard says.

Judy digs an elbow into Larrabee's ribs at that.

"But really! Music from *rocks!*" Simon exclaims.

Judy does not like Simon's tone of voice. "It so happens, Mr. Simon," she says indignantly, "that Howard has had discussions with Leonard Bernstein

56

about the possibility of conducting an avalanche. In E flat."

Simon slings his napkin on the table. "That is utterly ridiculous!" he says. His accent has thickened.

"I'll buy that," Judy agrees.

"Where's your sense of humor, Simon?" Larrabee asks, and then he turns to Howard. "She's a gem, Bannister. A gem. She's—unbelievable," Larrabee says passionately.

"I'll buy that," Howard agrees unhappily, shaking his head.

In the hotel lobby outside the banquet room, Eunice Burns is standing in front of the desk. A relief receptionist is on duty.

"What do you mean," Eunice is saying. "What do you mean when you say you can't find me? I'm right here."

"I'm sorry, Miss," the receptionist says. "I have no badge in that name."

"Well, look again, please. It's Burns. Miss Eunice Burns."

The receptionist checks the badges again, looks at Eunice and apologetically shakes her head in the negative.

Mr. Smith, carrying a paper bag from the coffee shop and several newspapers, walks across the lobby to the elevators. He has had a change of heart, and is now in a hurry to retrieve his overnight case and the documents. He rings for the elevator and pushes the button for the seventeenth floor when it arrives.

In room 1715, Harry sits on one of the twin beds. The closet door is open, and Harry is holding Smith's overnight case in his lap. He is talking into the telephone.

"*I've got the jewels,*" Harry says, a broad smile on his face.

Fritz, in the lobby, whispers back. "Get out of there, but don't let anyone see you," he instructs.

"Roger," Harry says.

"Fritz," says Fritz.

Harry hangs up and, taking the case, he leaves Mrs. Van Hoskins' room and steps out into the corridor. The elevator bell rings. Harry quickly fumbles for a passkey, crosses the hall to the nearest door, which is that of room 1714, opens the door and steps into Eunice's room just as the elevator door slides open.

Smith walks slowly from the elevator, looking at the front page of the top newspaper in his hands. He unlocks the door to room 1713 and goes inside. Now in his room, his nervousness lightens, and he decides there is time to eat his sandwich and read the papers before he retrieves his case. Smith settles in the easy chair beyond the twin beds.

In Eunice's room, Harry stands near the door, the purloined overnight case in his hand. He makes a sudden decision. There has been too much traffic in the 17th-floor corridor tonight to suit him. Bending over, he slides the case under the bed. Satisfied, Harry goes to the door, opens it a crack and peers out. The corridor is clear; the door to room 1713 is just closing. Harry leaves the overnight case under the bed, checks the number on the door, steps out into the corridor and heads for the elevators.

In the Bristol's banquet room, Simon and Larrabee are talking across Judy's back. Judy is leaning forward over her soup cup. Howard is signaling her.

"As you undoubtedly realize, Mr. Larrabee," Simon is saying, "I've spent almost six years on this latest study and I do feel that it is definitive."

"You've got to get out of here," Howard whispers urgently to Judy.

"And miss all the good stuff that's coming?" Judy whispers back.

"Eunice will be here any minute," Howard whispers urgently, pleading.

Judy grins at him impishly. "That's the good stuff that's coming," she whispers.

"Yes," Simon is saying. "I feel that my study is the definitive, even, if you will, the quintessential exegesis in terms of the Swiss composers and their. . . ."

"*Swiss* composers, Mr. Simon?" Judy interrupts.

"That's right, Miss Burns," Simon says.

Judy leans back in her chair, forcing Larrabee to lean forward. Howard leans back and signals at Judy, but she is listening to Simon now, and her back is to Howard.

Simon is talking to Judy in a patronizing manner. "I don't imagine it's a field that the musical—archae-ologists—find particularly interesting," he says, throwing a quick snide look at Howard. "But it's a rich field in which my ground-breaking scholarship has cultivated a rich harvest."

"That must have taken a lot of fertilizer," Judy tells Simon sweetly.

Larrabee laughs at her wit, to Simon's displeasure.

"I'd like to hear the story that Miss Burns . . . ." Larrabee begins to say.

"Burnsy," Judy interrupts.

Larrabee nods at her. "That Burnsy was telling to Professor Hosquith," Larrabee continues.

"He's calling her Burnsy," Howard says to himself in disbelief.

Larrabee turns to Howard. "What was it, Bannister," he asks. "Some adventure you had on your flight here?"

"Yes," Howard says automatically. "*No!*"

"I'm afraid my Howard is too modest to tell the story himself," Judy says, coming to the rescue. "But it all began shortly after we passed the point of no return."

"I think we just passed it," Howard says to himself.

Larrabee, and even Simon, are now listening to Judy attentively. Others at the table are also listening.

"At that point," Judy is saying, gesturing with her hands for emphasis, "the servo amplifiers and the directional gyro failed and the flux valve refused to disconnect. One of the pilots fainted from an over-supply of fear and we went into a power dive."

"I'm having a nightmare," Howard says to himself.

Judy continues the story dramatically. "Howard took his igneous rock formations into the cockpit and used two of them with a particularly high magnetic content to set up an electrically-induced field pattern on the gyrocompass and, just possibly, he was responsible for saving a hundred and twelve passengers from a tragic, fiery death." Judy throws out a hand toward Howard at the conclusion of her story, looking at him with an air of gratitude and love.

Larrabee settles back in his seat. "Absolutely incredible," he says, allowing himself to breathe again. He turns to Howard. "I find that story deeply moving," Larrabee says. "Allow me to shake your hand."

Howard nods his head unhappily and sticks out his hand.

Simon is staring at Judy over the top of his glasses. "I find that story as difficult to swallow as I do this *potage en gelée*," he says to her.

Sotto voce, she replies, "How would you like to swallow *une sandwiche de knuckles?*"

In the hotel lobby outside the banquet room, Eunice is standing in front of the desk. She is angry and is beginning to twitch. The receptionist has gone to fetch Mr. Butler, the head convention official, and now they return to the desk.

"What seems to be the problem?" Mr. Butler asks.

"This lady claims to be a Eunice Burns," the receptionist explains, "and . . . ."

"I am not *a* Eunice Burns," Eunice interrupts angrily. "I am *the* Eunice Burns."

"I have no badge for *a* Eunice Burns," the receptionist continues.

"Of course not," Mr. Butler says. "Miss Burns is wearing her badge. She has already gone into the banquet room and is sitting at the main table."

"That is impossible!" Eunice shrieks.

"Perhaps you're at the wrong convention," Mr. Butler says to Eunice kindly.

"*This is outrageous!*" Eunice proclaims in a shrill voice.

The official looks very unhappy.

Inside the banquet room, there is a lull between courses. Simon is talking to Professor Hosquith, sitting to his left and Larrabee has joined the conversation. He is leaning forward. Howard signals Judy. She nods, leans back, and they talk behind Larrabee's back.

"I have to speak with you privately," Howard pleads.

"Okay. Meet me under the table," Judy says.

"What?"

"Watch," she says. Judy pushes her napkin off her lap. "My goodness," she says loudly. "There goes my napkin." She slides off her seat after the napkin and disappears under the table.

Howard shrugs helplessly and follows her.

"So far, so good, huh? What's up, Doc?" Judy says. They are surrounded by a forest of legs.

"Don't you *understand* anything?" Howard asks Judy plaintively.

"Like what?" Judy asks.

"Like *Eunice*," Howard says patiently.

"Nope," Judy says. "I don't understand Eunice."

"She'll be here *any minute*."

"You've got to stop repeating yourself," Judy says.

"I'm not repeating myself," Howard says desperately. "I'm not repeating myself. Oh God—I'm repeating myself."

"Listen, Steve," Judy says seriously, "you don't want to marry Eunice."

"I'm not Steve. I'm *Howard*."

"Neither of you wants to marry Eunice," Judy says.

"Why do you say that?" Howard asks.

"You don't want to marry someone who's going to get all wrinkled and lined and flabby," Judy explains.

"Everyone gets wrinkled, lined and flabby," Howard says reasonably.

"By next week?" Judy asks.

Suddenly Larrabee's head appears underneath the table. "Say," he asks, "what's going on down here? Just can't keep away from each other, can you?" Larrabee gives a sympathetic little chuckle.

"Oh," Howard says lamely, "we were just talking."

Simon's head appears under the table. "Are you all right, Mr. Larrabee?" Simon asks. "Can I be of help?"

"No, no. I'm fine," Larrabee says. He slides under the table. "We're just chatting."

"About what?" Simon asks suspiciously, joining them.

"What's going on?" Professor Hosquith's head appears under the table. "Anything wrong?"

"No," Larrabee explains. "We were just chatting about, about . . . ."

"Just testing a theory Howard has about vocal reverberation under spinal pressure," Judy says.

Larrabee chuckles appreciatively. Howard groans.

"What?" Another head has appeared. "Vocal reverberation under spinal pressure?"

"V.R.U.S.P." Judy says.

"Of course," someone says.

"Oh yes, very interesting. I think I read a monograph on that," says a head from the end of the table.

Rudy, the headwaiter, has just entered the banquet room from the kitchen, and is directing the waiters to the tables. He looks at the main table, does a double take and summons the wine steward.

"Charles, what kind of wine are you serving at table one?" Rudy asks him.

Under the table, Larrabee pulls at Howard's sleeve. "I'm telling you, Bannister," he says to Howard, "this girl of yours is *fun*, F-U-N. And if you win the Larrabee grant, well, you can consider it her victory as well as your own. Do you follow me?"

"I-I," Howard stammers. He looks past Larrabee to Judy, who gives him a big wink and a smile. "I certainly do," Howard says hopelessly.

Simon snarls. Judy sticks out her tongue at him.

From the door of the banquet room coming from the hotel lobby are the sudden, loud sounds of a violent commotion. The door bursts open, and Eunice flings herself into the room. Her tic is twitching fiercely and her wig is vaguely askew. The receptionist, who is trying none too successfully to hold on to Eunice's arm, is being dragged across the polished banquet-room floor.

Everyone turns to look at Eunice. At the main table, Larrabee has flung up the front of the tablecloth to peer out. Howard sees Eunice, and tries gamely to hide behind Larrabee's back.

"Howard! Howard Bannister!" Eunice shrieks.

Rudy and several of his staff begin closing in on

63

Eunice, whose arms are waving wildly. The receptionist is now protecting her head.

"Howard! Where are you? Tell them who I am!" Eunice raves. "They're trying to keep me out. They won't believe me!"

"Who is that dangerously unbalanced woman?" Larrabee asks in awe.

Howard looks at Larrabee, his mouth open. Eunice spots Howard under the table and bends down. "Howard, I insist you tell them who I am. Howard, I insist you tell them who I am, right this minute," Eunice shrieks. "Right this minute!"

Eunice's tic has assumed epic proportions. *"Tell them who I am, Howard!"*

Howard turns away helplessly and looks at Judy for help.

"Tell them, Howard," Judy says.

Everyone under the table is looking at Howard.

"I never saw her before in my life," Howard says.

Judy smiles innocently.

Two waiters, the receptionist, Rudy and Mr. Butler, the banquet official, drag Eunice backward out of the room. Her high heels leave little skid marks on the polished floor. The banquet guests are silent, watching the door through which Eunice has been taken.

Howard is in shock.

Judy reaches out and pats him reassuringly on the cheek.

CHAPTER SIX

It is midnight. In the banquet room a waiter is removing the American Musicologists' Convention banner from the wall and folding it carefully. Judy and Howard, alone at the main banquet table, watch him silently. Judy is still hungry. Howard slumps in his chair, his face mirroring the ordeal he has just endured. The waiter nods good-night to them, and takes the banner out of the banquet hall to the storage room. The dishes have been cleared from the table, and Howard and Judy sit looking at the tablecloth, which bears spotted remains of the banquet. Judy moves into the chair recently vacated by Larrabee and puts her hand on Howard's arm.

"What's the matter, Steve?" Judy asks him.

"My name is not Steve," Howard says, pulling his arm away, "and the matter is how I'm going to explain all this to Eunice."

"Oh, that's the easiest thing in the world," Judy says.

Judy turns Howard around to face her, suddenly serious, and Howard listens to her now intently.

"Obviously, you have no understanding of women," Judy continues. "You go right to her room and knock on the door. She will answer the door."

Howard nods in agreement.

"She will have been crying," Judy tells him, "so her nose will be all red and runny and her eyes puffy and bloodshot. But you'll overlook that."

Howard grimaces, but nods in agreement anyway.

"You'll put your hand on her shoulder," Judy instructs, "softly yet firmly, stare purposefully into those red rimmed swollen eyes and say in a calm, masculine voice: 'Eunice, my dear, there has been a terrible misunderstanding.'"

Howard is slowly looking relieved, silently repeating Judy's words to himself.

"And then you'll say," Judy continues, "'I have acted like a cad—a bounder—but now I see everything clearly and I have decided that Judy and I are going to put you in a home.'"

Howard stares at Judy for a long time. Slowly, he shakes his head. "That is not amusing," he says sadly.

"Look," Judy says, "I don't know what you're so miserable about. Tonight was a victory. We've got the Larrabee grant virtually sewn up."

"We?" Howard exclaims.

"Well, you have to admit I helped," Judy points out. "After all, he calls me Burnsy."

"That is not the point," Howard replies. "You are not Burnsy. Burnsy is Burnsy. I mean—Eunice is Burnsy. I mean she isn't Burnsy. No one is Burnsy," he finishes lamely, putting his head in his hands.

"So, what is the point?" Judy asks.

"The point is. . . ." Howard sits up and stares out into the empty banquet room. "The point is. . . . Oh God, I've forgotten the point." Howard looks at Judy helplessly.

"The point is," Judy tells him, "that you think that when Mr. Larrabee finds out that I'm not Eunice, he'll think that you tried to put something over on him and it's bye-bye twenty thousand smackeroos."

"That's it!" Howard agrees. "That's the point. That money will help me to establish certain proofs for theories of mine—certain theories that. . . ."

Judy has moved in very close to Howard, rapt with attention, staring directly into his eyes.

"Look," Howard asks, "could you not sit quite so close?"

"I'm very nearsighted," Judy says.

"Where was I?" Howard asks, moving over one chair to his right.

"Certain theories," Judy says, following him.

"Right. That money would enable me to travel to certain sites in the south of France to examine evidence of prehistoric art forms hundreds of thousands of years old," Howard explains.

"Aurignacian or Upper Perigordian?" Judy asks.

"Well, both actually," Howard says seriously, "if I can have the opportunity to. . . ." He stops. "Where do you come up with those names?"

"Just a wild guess," Judy says, shrugging her shoulders.

Judy leans close to him again, and with sudden determination Howard stands up and, taking Judy firmly by the arm, he leads her across the banquet room to the door to the hotel lobby. Judy drags behind him reluctantly.

Howard opens the door to the lobby. "I want you to go away now," he tells Judy.

Judy steps out into the lobby, takes a few steps then turns and comes back. She is looking solemn. She reaches out and puts her hand on Howard's arm. "Steve," she says, "I'm sorry. I only wanted to help."

Howard is moved and slightly embarrassed. "Well," he tells her, "I—I know you didn't mean any harm. You're just—just different."

"Thank you. I know I'm different. But I'm going to try to become the same."

"The same as what?" Howard asks.

"The same as people who aren't different."

"Good," Howard says. "Thank you—and good-bye."

"Aww—give me a chance, Steve," Judy begs. "When you get to know me better, you'll really like me."

"I won't like you," Howard says. "Good-bye."

Judy thinks about it for a minute, playing with the lapel of Howard's dinner jacket.

"Let's not say good-bye," she suggests finally. "Let's just say *au revoir*."

Howard thinks about that for a moment. "No," he says. "Let's say good-bye." Firmly he removes Judy's hand from his jacket, turns her around and propels her out the door, shutting it behind him. Absently, he turns back into the banquet room and begins to take off his jacket, moving to the center of the empty room. Suddenly he realizes where he is. He shakes his head, sighs, and readjusts his jacket.

Fritz and Harry are standing near the desk in the lobby, trying to maintain an innocuous air to their conversation as guests pass by, or occasionally stop to get a room key.

"Look," Fritz says, spying Mrs. Van Hoskins being helped from the back seat of a Rolls Royce by a long-haired smiling young man; the Rolls has stopped directly in front of the Bristol's main door. "Here she comes now. Did you get the jewels out of the hotel?" Fritz asks Harry.

"I didn't have time," Harry says. "I put the overnight case in room seventeen-fourteen."

"Seventeen-fourteen?" Fritz exclaims. What kind of a house detective are you that you cannot commit a simple burglary?"

"I'm ashamed," Harry admits, hanging his head.

"Never mind," Fritz says. "I will return the case to Mrs. Van Hoskins' room while you detain her. Can you do that?" Fritz asks.

"How do I do that?" Harry asks.

"Use your charm," Fritz tells him. He turns on his heel and goes to the elevator, leaving an unhappy Harry watching Mrs. Van Hoskins and William Lockland III slowly enter the hotel. "Charm. Use your charm," Harry repeats to himself.

Judy stands momentarily in the hotel lobby, wondering if she should rejoin Howard in the banquet room. Suddenly she smiles, opens her bag and extracts a room key. Judy crosses the lobby and enters the elevators, humming softly.

In room 1714, Eunice is sitting at the dressing table, her head resting on her arms to keep a large, wet towel in place on her twitching forehead. Her evening dress is thrown carelessly on the floor between the beds. Finally, she pulls herself together enough to get into her bathrobe and retrieve her dress from the floor and hang it in the closet. She moves Howard's overnight case, which had been under her dress between the beds, to the foot of the far twin bed, rewets the cloth for her forehead and lies down to rest.

Howard leaves the banquet room, finally, crosses the lobby, and waits for an elevator to take him to the seventeenth floor. He wonders if he can postpone his confrontation with Eunice until the morning.

William Lockland and Mrs. Van Hoskins are saying a long, fond good-evening in the hotel lobby, watched carefully by Harry. "Use your charm," Harry reminds himself. Finally, William Lockland raises Mrs. Van Hoskins' hand to his lips for a good-night kiss, and he leaves the hotel. Mrs. Van Hoskins waits until the

Rolls drives off, then starts slowly across the lobby toward the elevator.

Fritz stands in front of room 1714. He listens at the door for a moment, then knocks gently. There is no reply. He knocks again, louder.

"What do you want?" Eunice answers. Her voice is unsteady.

"Madame," Fritz says, "it is I, Fritz, of the Hotel Bristol's staff."

The door opens. Eunice has her damp cloth pressed to her forehead. She is looking horrendous.

"I suppose you've come to apologize," Eunice says, "for the unbelievable, criminal injustices that have been visited upon me in this place." Emotion overcomes Eunice, and she can not go on. She retreats into the room, sits on a bed, and hides her face in her hands. Fritz looks hungrily at the overnight case on the floor before the far bed.

"No, Miss Burns, that's not it. The fact is, one of our guests has lost something," Fritz says.

"Well, Mr. Fritz," Eunice says sarcastically, "I fail to see how it could possibly be in here unless it *crawled* in, under its own power."

Fritz's eyes light up. "Exactly, Miss Burns," he says.

"What are you trying to say?" Eunice asks.

"It's very embarrassing," Fritz says. "But one of our regular guests—a wealthy eccentric—has lost his pet snake." Fritz spreads his hands and then clasps them at his chest, as if asking for understanding.

Eunice screams and leaps onto the bed.

"May I suggest that you shut yourself in the bathroom for a few minutes while I search the room?" Fritz crosses the room and opens the bathroom door, bowing to Eunice to enter.

"What if it's in there?" Eunice asks weakly.

Fritz thinks quickly. "No. It won't be in there,

70

Miss Burns," he assures her. "Snakes, as you know, live in mortal fear of—of *tile*," he says triumphantly.

Eunice stares at Fritz, nods, leaps off the bed and rushes into the bathroom, slamming the door behind her. Fritz immediately moves around to the far bed, picks up Howard's overnight case from the floor and carries it back to the door. He steps into the corridor and calls out to Eunice.

"It is all right, Miss Burns. You may come out now." Fritz closes the door to room 1714 and quickly crosses the hall to room 1715, carrying the overnight case containing Howard's igneous rock formations. He takes out his passkey and enters Mrs. Van Hoskins' room.

Eunice is cowering behind the bathroom door, a fresh wet cloth on her forehead. She opens the door to her room cautiously and peeks out. Fritz has left. Slowly she crosses the bathroom threshhold, belts her bathrobe firmly and rushes to the bed. "What more can they do to me?" she asks herself plaintively.

Mrs. Van Hoskins has half crossed the hotel lobby, and is now level with Harry.

"Charm," Harry says to himself. "Use your charm. . . ."

As Mrs. Van Hoskins' steps pass him, Harry sticks out a foot and trips her. She goes down like a whale. All apologies, Harry bends down to help her up, but Mrs. Van Hoskins indignantly pushes him away, gets up and continues to the elevator. Harry follows her.

The elevator door opens on the 17th floor. Mrs. Van Hoskins quickly leaves the elevator, with Harry in pursuit. Outside the door to room 1710, Harry trips her. Quickly Mrs. Van Hoskins bites his leg and holds on.

The door to room 1715 opens and Fritz steps out

cautiously. Harry escapes Mrs. Van Hoskins, and he and Fritz ride the elevator to the main floor.

In room 1717, Jones suddenly jerks awake, stretches and feels the overnight case on the bed beside him. "Ahh" he murmurs to himself. "The documents." Jones lights a match and checks the time on his watch.

In room 1714, Eunice is sitting up in bed, reading *The Sensuous Woman*. The wet cloth is gone from her forehead, but her face still is looking tense. Suddenly she slams the manual shut. She has at least expected Howard to come to her room and offer an apology. Eunice gets out of bed, leans down to pick up Howard's overnight case from the foot of the far twin bed, and looks around, puzzled. The case is not there. She gets on her hands and knees to check under the beds and pulls out an overnight case. It is Smith's case of documents, pushed under the bed by Harry, who thought it was Mrs. Van Hoskins' jewelry. Eunice puts the case on her bed and ponders it, rubbing her fingers cautiously over her eye. She wonders why she put the case under the bed. She can't remember.

The door to room 1717 opens, and Jones peers into the corridor. His golf bag is in one hand; Mrs. Van Hoskins' overnight case is in the other.

Eunice opens the door to room 1714 and peers out into the corridor; the overnight case from under the bed is in her hand.

Jones quickly closes the door to his room and, with a sigh of resignation, he goes back to the bed and lies down with the case of jewelry on his chest.

Eunice, carrying the case she believes contains Howard's rock formations, tiptoes to the door of room 1716. She raises her hand to knock, changes her mind, puts the case on the floor in front of Howard's door and, with an angry twitch of her head, she goes back to her room and closes the door behind her.

72

The elevator door opens, and Howard comes into the corridor. He is looking in his pockets for his key. He walks slowly to his room, stops and looks down at the case on the floor outside his door, makes a step toward Eunice's room, changes his mind and picks up the case. He cannot find his key. He tries the door. It is open. Howard takes the case into his room and puts it on the dresser.

Fritz and Harry stand in the deserted lobby. Fritz is giving Harry instructions; Harry is listening attentively.

"You will enter Mrs. Van Hoskins' room through the adjoining room, take the jewel case and go straight to the basement with it," Fritz says.

"What if she wakes up and sees me?" Harry asks.

"You will tell her that you are smitten by her, that you have followed her all night and you will make passionate love to her," Fritz says.

Harry thinks about it a moment. "Couldn't I just kill her?" he asks.

Fritz looks at him sternly. Harry shrugs.

In room 1716, Howard has removed his formal jacket and thrown it over a chair. He now stands before the bureau mirror, trying to undo his plaid bowtie. It doesn't untie. Furiously, Howard rips at the tie, almost strangling himself. It won't come undone. He unbuttons his shirt and pulls the collar out from under the bowtie, takes off his shirt and throws it on top of his jacket. With a sigh, he sits on the bed, removes his shoes, takes off his pants and starts to take off his shorts.

"Hello, out there," Judy says.

"Hello," Howard answers automatically. He freezes. "It must be brain damage," he says to himself.

"What?" Judy's voice is coming from the bathroom. Deeply horrified, Howard rummages in the open

73

suitcase on his bed, finds a pair of pajama bottoms, pulls them on over his shorts and, holding them up with his hands, he cautiously approaches the bathroom.

Howard slowly pushes open the bathroom door, stands in the doorway and stares, mouth open.

Judy is in the bathtub, covered to her neck by a bubble bath. Her overnight case is closed, and sits on the floor under the sink. Her street clothes are pushed into the towel rack.

Howard trembles, puts his hands out to balance himself against the door jamb, and his pajama pants drop around his socks, exposing his shorts.

Judy looks him up and down. "I believe you dropped something, Steve," she says sweetly.

"What do you think you're doing?"

"I think I'm taking a bath. Aren't I?" Judy says.

Howard, exasperated, turns around in a circle, getting tangled in his pajama bottoms. He steps out of them, straightens the legs, and begins to put them back on.

"If you're not out of here in two minutes, I'm going to call the police," Howard warns.

"Who do you think they'll arrest, Steve," Judy asks reasonably, "the girl in the tub or the guy with his pants down?"

"I'm not joking now," Howard says, his face beginning to turn red. "I don't like to act rashly but you are the last straw that breaks my camel's back. You—you—you're a plague," he says, gesturing with both hands, causing his pajama bottoms to fall again around his socks. "You bring havoc and chaos to everyone," Howard continues, undaunted. "But why to me? *Why me? Why me? Why? Why?*"

"Because you look cute in your red plaid bowtie

74

and pajama bottoms, Steve," Judy says. "Or out of them. . . ."

"Get out! You've got to *get out!*" Howard's voice is rising shrilly.

"Right now?" Judy asks.

"Yes," he says emphatically.

Judy starts to get out of the bathtub.

"No! Wait a minute!" Howard backs out of the bathroom, trips on his pajama bottoms and falls heavily on his back onto the floor.

"Are you all right?" Judy calls. She splashes her way out of the tub.

"I don't know. I think I've broken several major bones," Howard says, awkwardly trying to get up off the floor.

Judy appears in the bathroom doorway, wrapped in a large towel, and drying her hair with a second. She looks down at Howard.

"Let me see," she says.

"Don't help me," Howard pleads. "Please don't help me. I can do without your help."

"Just tell me where it hurts," Judy asks. "Is it the ilium? The sacrum? The coccyx? I hope it's not your coccyx."

"I can't seem to breathe," Howard says. "Is it possible to break a lung?"

"I think your bowtie is too tight," Judy says.

Howard works at the tie frantically, and finally gets it somewhat loosened.

The phone rings.

"There!" Howard says. "Now the phone is ringing!"

"I'll get it," Judy offers.

"NO! No—I can do it." Howard crawls to the phone, pulling on the cord and toppling it to the floor.

"Hello. Yes," Howard says into the phone. "Eunice who? Oh—Eunice."

"Howard, what's going on in there?" Eunice asks. She is sitting up in bed by the phone in her room.

"Nothing much," Howard says, cradling the phone against his shoulder and tying his pajama pants. "I fell down, that's all."

"Are you hurt?" Eunice asks.

"Oh no. I feel much better now. Thank you for calling." Howard starts to hang up.

"*Howard!*" Eunice yells.

"Yes, Eunice." Howard puts the receiver back to his ear.

"I'm coming in there," Eunice tells him.

"I wish you wouldn't, Eunice." Howard has retrieved his pajama top from the suitcase and is struggling into it. Judy walks over to help with the buttons and Howard waves her away in exasperation.

"Well, I want to see if you're all right," Eunice is saying. "I'm still very angry with you, but I *am* concerned." She pauses, waiting for Howard to reply. "Do you hear me, Howard?" Eunice asks.

"Yes. But. . . ."

"I think I'll get dressed," Judy says.

"Howard, who was that?" Eunice asks, sitting bolt upright in the bed.

"Who was what?" Howard asks innocently.

"I heard a voice say something about getting dressed," Eunice says.

Howard reaches over and turns on the television set. He shakes a fist at Judy.

"It's the television, dear," Howard tells Eunice. "There's a movie on." A war movie appears on the television screen. "They're getting dressed for the big battle."

"It was a *woman's* voice," Eunice says.

"Uh—they're lady soldiers, Eunice. It's called 'The Fighting WAC'S,' " Howard says desperately.

"You don't have a bathrobe I could put on, do you, Steve?" Judy asks Howard.

"I'm coming in there!" Eunice shrieks and hangs up the phone.

"Well—that's it," Howard says. "There's only one thing left to do." Howard walks to the window, opens it and starts to climb out.

"What are you doing?" Judy asks.

"Eunice is coming," Howard explains calmly. "You're here—in your—towel—and I'm going to jump. Good-bye."

"Steve!" Judy rushes over, grabs Howard by his pajama bottoms and pulls. They both fall backward onto the floor. The pajama pants rip.

Howard turns around to look at the damage. "I don't believe it," he says. "You did it again." He reaches for his tuxedo pants and starts to put them on over his pajamas.

Eunice's tic has started twitching once again. She stands for a moment staring at the phone in her hand, then gets into her bathrobe and purposely she enters the corridor, leaving her door ajar. She walks down the hall and knocks loudly on the door to Howard's room.

"Open this door, Howard," Eunice demands.

The elevator door opens and Harry steps out into the 17th floor corridor.

In room 1717, Jones hears the commotion in the hall and opens his door a crack to listen. He sees Harry coming down the hall and Eunice standing in the corridor.

Eunice stops Harry. "Excuse me, are you with the hotel?" she asks him.

"Why?" Harry asks suspiciously.

77

"I'd like the key to this room," Eunice explains, pointing to the door to 1716. "My fiance is in there and I believe he has injured himself."

"Sorry, lady," Harry tells her. "I'm looking for something in seventeen-seventeen."

"Yes," Eunice begins, "but. . . ."

Harry shakes his head and pushes past Eunice.

In room 1717, Jones looks desperately around for a place to hide. He rejects the closet, rushes across to the window and opens it. He picks up his golf bag and the Van Hoskins overnight case, climbs onto the ledge outside, closes the window behind him and starts edging his way along the ledge until he is out of sight of the window.

Eunice knocks on Howard's door loudly. "Open this door immediately," she says.

The door to room 1713 opens a crack, and Smith peers out into the hall. He leaves his door ajar, and keeps his eye on Eunice.

In room 1716, Howard is pulling Judy out of the closet. He is looking over his shoulder at the door, where Eunice is now knocking rhythmically.

"What's wrong with the closet?" Judy asks.

"She'll look in there," Howard explains.

"What kind of person *is* she?" Judy asks indignantly.

The door to room 1710 opens, and Hugh Simon, dressed in pajamas, looks out and down the hall. As he sees Eunice, and hears her calling Howard, a look of speculation appears on his face. He puts a finger to his mouth thoughtfully, closes his door and leans against it, thinking hard.

Eunice's voice has gotten shriller. "Howard Bannister," she says loudly, "I'm talking to you."

Howard is looking out the window. He holds Judy by the arm. She is trying to pull away.

78

"No, no, I can't do it. I'm terrified of heights," Judy says in terror. "I have acrophobia."

"Look," Howard says reasonably, "there's a ledge."

"I have ledgeophobia," Judy says.

Howard pushes her toward the window. "Just until I can get rid of Eunice," he promises.

"I can't," Judy says.

"Howard!" Eunice shrieks from the hall.

"She has a violent temper," Howard explains to Judy.

"I can't," Judy says, trying to back away from the window.

"Howard!" Eunice's voice has gotten nasty.

"She studies karate," Howard tells Judy.

"Maybe I can," Judy agrees.

Howard helps Judy out the window and onto the ledge.

"I'm going to count to five, Howard," Eunice warns, pounding on the door.

"Don't count, Eunice. I hate it when you count," Howard calls to Eunice. He pats Judy reassuringly on the arm, closes the window and quickly puts his tuxedo jacket back on.

Judy, on the ledge, opens the window. Howard struggles with her.

"One!" Eunice counts.

Howard gets the window closed and begins to button and straighten his clothes.

"Two!"

"Three!"

Howard races to the bathroom, retrieves Judy's clothes from the towel rack, throws them into his suitcase on the bed and slams it shut. With a last desperate look at the window, he runs across the room to the door.

"Four!" Eunice yells.

Howard yanks open the door.

"Five!" Eunice shrieks.

"Hi, Eunice," Howard says. "Come on in."

Harry, who has stood in the hall to watch the spectacle, now unlocks the door to room 1717 with his passkey. He walks immediately to the connecting door to Mrs. Van Hoskins' room and listens. Miraculously, there is the faint sound of snoring. Harry unlocks the connecting door as quietly as he can.

In room 1710, Hugh Simon is slipping into his monogrammed bathrobe, about to enter the hall to see what is going on. A look of anticipation is on his face.

In room 1713, Smith is pacing the floor. He has shut his door and is evaluating the disturbance in the hall, trying to figure out how it may apply to him. He decides it is time to retrieve his overnight case and the documents from the closet in the adjoining room.

The connecting door opens quietly, and from room 1717, Harry quickly scurries into Mrs. Van Hoskins' room. He carefully makes his way to the bureau, lifts the overnight case containing Howard's rocks and then crawls with it back through the connecting door, closing and locking it behind him.

Eunice has walked directly to Howard's closet and opened the door. Howard stands behind her, smiling nervously.

"Howard," Eunice says, "if you have betrayed my trust in you. . . ." Satisfied that the closet is empty, she closes the closet, walks to the bathroom and opens the door. "If you—*what's that?*" Eunice asks shrilly.

Howard looks in. Eunice is pointing to the bathtub.

"That's a bath, Eunice," Howard says. "I was going to take a bath."

"Since when have you taken *bubble baths*, Howard?"

"It came out of the faucet that way," Howard says.

Eunice looks at the overnight case under the sink. "Why are your rocks in the bathroom, Howard?" Eunice asks.

"I don't know," Howard sighs. "I wish I did, but I don't." He takes Judy's case and brings it out into the bedroom.

The connecting door to room 1715 from room 1713 opens and Smith comes into Mrs. Van Hoskins' room on his hands and knees. He crawls quickly to the closet, reaches up and opens the door. He stands and feels frantically about for his overnight case. It is not there. He crawls to the corridor door, opens it a crack and peers out. Behind him in the bed, Mrs. Van Hoskins is snoring soundly.

At the end of the hall opposite the elevators, Jones is inching his way carefully along the outside ledge, carrying the overnight case filled with Mrs. Van Hoskins' jewelry, and his golf bag. Jones stops and tries to open the window at the end of the hall, but it is locked. He grimaces and moves on down the ledge and out of sight. Smith watches him go with mounting fury.

Mrs. Van Hoskins gives a groan and turns over in her sleep. Smith freezes, then dashes into the corridor, closing the door quietly, and across it to enter Eunice's room. She has left her door open. He heads for the window, pulls back the drapes and peers cautiously out to the ledge. Jones is inching his way toward the window of room 1714, where Smith is standing. Smith lets the drapes fall and steps back, satisfied.

On the ledge outside room 1716, Judy is freezing. She huddles close to the window, wrapped in her towel, balancing from one foot to the other to keep warm, humming softly to herself to pass the time.

The door to room 1717 opens and Harry cautiously peeks into the corridor. It is empty. He enters the hall quickly, carrying Howard's overnight case. Harry closes the door behind him and runs down the corridor heading for the elevators.

The elevator bell rings.

Harry pulls out his passkey, opens the door to room 1711 and goes in, shutting the door behind him.

The elevator door opens and a waiter, wheeling a cart, walks out and starts briskly up the corridor.

In room 1716, Eunice is on her hands and knees, looking under a bed.

"What are you looking for, dear?" Howard asks her nervously. Judy is struggling with the window from outside on the ledge, and Howard rushes over and draws the curtains in front of the window.

Eunice stands up. "Howard," she says, "you are *not* being open with me," she complains.

"Eunice, I *am* being open with you," Howard says. "I am *always* open."

There is a knock on the door.

"It's open," Howard continues.

The waiter walks in cheerfully. "Where do you want it, ma'am?" he asks Eunice.

"Where do I want *what?*" Eunice asks.

"Roast beef on rye," the waiter says, pointing to his tray, "mustard on top . . . ."

"*I don't want food!*" Eunice screams.

"Room seventeen-sixteen, right?" the waiter says. "Well, I'll just set it up over here." Not paying the slightest attention to anything else going on, the waiter happily wheels the cart to a corner.

Judy is very cold, and beginning to get frightened. She is holding onto the window frame, trying to keep her balance and the towel wrapped around her at the same time. She raps lightly on the window to attract Howard's attention.

"What's that?" Eunice asks.

"What's *what?*" Howard says innocently.

"I heard knocking," Eunice insists.

Howard turns up the television volume. "It's your nerves, dear," he tells Eunice.

Outside, on the ledge, Judy reaches down, opens the window and slowly begins climbing back into the room.

Eunice has stopped flailing around momentarily, her attention on a cold cream commercial. With horror, Howard glances at the window. A leg is sticking through the drapes. He cautiously backs to the window, reaches through the curtains, and none too gently pushes Judy back outside to the ledge. Howard shuts the window as quietly as he can and readjusts the drapes.

Judy loses her balance, and with a little screech, she falls off the ledge, grabbing it as she goes down and managing barely to hang on. She just manages to clutch the towel under her chin.

"Why are you fiddling with the window, Howard?" Eunice asks, inside the room. The commercial over, she is surveying the room for other places to check. She opens the closet door again. Howard turns up the television volume a bit.

"Too much fresh air, dear," Howard tells her. "Very harmful."

Hugh Simon has left room 1710 and now moves stealthily along the corridor. His bathrobe is firmly belted at his waist and he wears bedroom slippers. He has begun to put two and two together, and has decided that if he is right it will add up to $20,000. He licks his lips in anticipation.

Eunice is standing in the middle of room 1716,

hands on her hips, glowering at Howard. "Will you, for goodness sake, turn off that television," she demands.

"Yes, Eunice." Howard has moved back to the window, ready to intercept Judy if she attempts to open the window once again.

In the hall outside, Simon is bent over, his ear to the door of room 1716. At the sound of the name "Eunice," he straightens up. A look of utterly smug satisfaction crosses his face, he wrings his hands in glee and quickly returns down the hall to room 1710, almost skipping with pleasure. "Eunice," he says to himself.

His eyes still on the window, Howard backs to the television set, reaches down for the volume knob, and turns it the wrong way. It comes off in his hand. He stares at it in anguish. The television set blares an aspirin commercial at top volume.

"Howard, if you don't turn that set off, I am going to scream," Eunice yells.

"You are screaming, Eunice," Howard yells back.

In room 1711, Harry stands with his ear to the door, listening to the muted sounds of a commotion further down the hall. He opens the door a crack, and hears the blaring television set. He crosses to the telephone and calls the lobby to report to Fritz, eyeing the overnight case on the floor.

"Fritz," Fritz says.

"This is Harry. I'm in room 1711. Something noisy is going on down the hall. I have the case. What shall I do?" Harry asks.

"I don't know. I have had three complaints from rooms on the eighteenth floor," Fritz tells Harry. He thinks about it. "Hide the case and go see what is going on," he says finally. "I'll be up in a minute."

"Roger," Harry tells him.

"Fritz."

Harry looks around the room for a place to hide the case from Mrs. Van Hoskins' room. Finally, he pushes it under the far twin bed and replaces the bedspread carefully. Satisfied, he starts for the door.

Eunice and Howard stand in the middle of the floor in room 1716, looking up. The light fixture is shimmying. The people in the room above are banging furiously on the floor.

The phone starts ringing.

"Pull the television plug out, Howard," Eunice yells.

"It's a cable."

"Pull the cable out."

The waiter, long finished setting the table, has been waiting patiently, pencil and bill in hand. Now Howard waves him away and goes to take a look at the television cable.

Jones, overnight bag in one hand, golf bag in the other, has now inched his way around the hotel's 17th floor ledge until he is nearly to the outside of the window of room 1716. He can hear the commotion. He does not look down. His face is red and beads of sweat are on his forehead. He stops outside the window, and tries to peer through the draperies to see what is happening in the room.

Judy, hanging precariously from the ledge, readjusts her position, and with a great effort she reaches up and grabs the ankle that has appeared on the ledge above her head.

With a terrified shriek, Jones falls against the window.

Judy manages to gain a foothold on the ledge.

Howard yanks the television cable with all his might. It rips out of the wall, sending a torrent of sparks throughout the room as Jones comes crashing through the window. His golf bag falls to the floor at his feet and Mrs. Van Hoskins' overnight case shoots out of his hand and under the closer of the two twin beds.

Eunice screams.

The waiter offers her the pencil and bill. She pushes him away. Smoke begins to fill the room from several small fires started by the sparks from the cable. Howard anxiously starts putting out a fire on the drapes. The waiter, looking around the damage in the room and anxious to be gone, presents the bill to Jones, who pushes him away in disgust, frantically looking around for the case.

Smith, who has watched Jones' progress on the ledge through the curtains in room 1714, now quietly opens the connecting door from Eunice's room, unnoticed in the commotion. The door half open, Smith spots Judy's overnight case close-by. He reaches out a hand, grabs the case and drags it back into room 1714, closing the connecting door behind him.

Howard and Eunice are trying to put out the fires in the room. Eunice's bathrobe is beginning to smoke. The waiter hands her a glass of water and the bill.

Harry has entered the corridor from room 1711, and now hurries to the door of room 1716. Smoke is coming into the corridor from beneath the door. He takes out his passkey, opens the door and quickly throws it open, standing speechless, momentarily, at the spectacle in the room.

"Somebody's under arrest!" Harry screams.

Fritz, coming down the hall from the elevators, now joins Harry in the doorway. Harry looks at Fritz and nods. Fritz nods back. Harry nods. Fritz nods, then pushes Harry away in disgust and walks into the room. He looks around in horror, then begins to help put out the fires. The waiter offers him the bill.

Smith now darts out of room 1714 and down the

hall into his room, 1713, closing the door behind him, the overnight case in his hand. He stands resting against the door.

The elevator door opens and a squad of firemen rush out and down the corridor to room 1716. Smoke now is billowing into the corridor from the open door. The waiter steps into the hall and hands his bill to the fire chief.

Judy steps through the broken window into room 1716, her towel wrapped around her. Through the smoke and confusion, she walks over to Eunice. "Why, Miss Burns," Judy says sweetly. "What are you doing in Mr. Bannister's bedroom? Don't you know the meaning of *propriety?*"

Eunice begins twitching wildly.

CHAPTER SEVEN

False dawn is breaking over San Francisco. On a street nearby the hotel, a taxicab cruises slowly, its headlights yellow in the early morning haze. On a green park bench, Jones sits up, awakened by the noise. His golf bag is across his lap. The one remaining club has had its head half burned away, and it is smoking slightly. There are several charred spots on the bag, and Jones examines them ruefully. His head nods forward in sleep once again and he jerks it back, rubbing his eyes. He checks his watch, and then stares grimly at the hotel. He had had the documents right in his hands! The Chief will not be pleased.

Harry has spent the night in room 1711, the overnight case he had taken from Mrs. Van Hoskins' room on the bed beside him. The phone rings once, a reminder from Fritz in the lobby. Harry awakens, remembers where he is, takes the overnight case and checking to see that the corridor is clear, he quickly walks to the elevators and rides to the basement of the hotel. With his passkey Harry opens the door to the hotel's utility room and secures Howard's overnight case on a shelf behind a pile of cartons. He locks the door behind himself, and takes the elevator to the lobby. He has not been seen. Fritz will be pleased.

In room 1715, Mrs. Van Hoskins is still asleep and snoring slightly. The overnight case on her bureau is gone. Mrs. Van Hoskins will not be happy.

In room 1714, Eunice Burns is asleep, a black sleep mask over her eyes. At the foot of the bed is *The Sensuous Woman,* which she had tossed aside the previous evening. She turns in her sleep, restless. Above the top of the sleep mask, at irregular intervals, her tic is still active.

In room 1713, Smith is sitting in a chair, looking haggard. He is staring at Judy's overnight case on the floor nearby. At his feet is a disorderly pile of newspaper pages and the wrinkled paper bag that had contained his sandwich the night before. He has made a quick trip to the hotel's lobby and bought two packs of cigarettes which he is patiently smoking. He had not smoked in two years. Smith's doctor will not be happy.

In room 1710, Hugh Simon is asleep, smiling broadly. On the pillow near his head is an invitation to lunch with Mr. Larrabee and although the note made no mention of the grant money, Simon is now convinced that it is his. "Eunice," he murmurs in his sleep. The members of the Conservatory will be very pleased.

In room 1716, Howard Bannister is lying on one of the beds, still dressed in his banquet clothes, with a partially burned bedspread pulled over himself. He is asleep. There is a knock on the door. Howard sits up groggily, picks up the phone receiver and says hello. The operator asks him for his call. He stares at the phone. There is another knock at the door, which causes the handle to fall off onto the floor. Howard replaces the receiver.

"Come in, it's broken," Howard says. "I mean, it's open." He puts his feet on the floor, tossing off the bedspread.

Mr. Kaltenborn, the manager of the hotel, cautiously pushes open the door. He stands absolutely still in the doorway, looking at the room in horror. Mr. Kaltenborn is not happy.

"Good morning," Howard says, trying to be cheerful.

"No, I don't think so. I'm Mr. Kaltenborn, the manager of what's left of this hotel." Kaltenborn, now getting a closer look at the damage in the room, appears as if he might faint.

The room is an unbelievable sight. The window is broken and glass shards glitter all over the rug. The draperies are half burned away and are still smoldering; water from the firemen's hoses drips from the wall fixtures and has saturated the spread on the bed next to the television set. Lamps and chairs are overturned and the busted cable of the television set is still smoking. The heavy smell of water-quenched fire is in the air, and scorched places mar the rug permanently.

"I'm awfully sorry about this whole mess here," Howard apologizes. "Usually, this doesn't happen."

"Dr. Bannister," Kaltenborn says, finding his voice, "I have a message for you from the staff of the hotel."

"Really? What is it?"

"Good-bye." Kaltenborn has clenched his hands together, as if to keep them from adding to the violence in the room.

"That's the entire message?" Howard asks.

"No. We would appreciate it if you would check out."

"When?" Howard asks.

"Yesterday," Kaltenborn tells him.

"That soon?" Howard says with a sigh of resignation. "Listen, I don't suppose there's another room you could let me have for a few. . . ." Howard stops as he sees the expression of utter disbelief on Kaltenborn's face.

"Ahh, well. . . ." Howard, resigned, breathes deeply and looks around for his shoes. They are under the bed, next to Mrs. Van Hoskins' overnight case, which had flown out of Jones' hand when he fell through the window. Howard pulls out the case.

"These are my igneous tambula drums," Howard explains to Kaltenborn, holding the case close to his chest, beneath his bow tie.

"Yes, of course they are," Kaltenborn says, carefully, as if confronted with a madman.

Howard puts on his shoes, and taking the overnight case he goes out into the hall. Kaltenborn, with another horrified look around the room, follows Howard and pulls the door closed behind them. The other half of the door handle comes off in his hand.

They walk silently to the elevator, Howard carrying the overnight case, Kaltenborn carefully carrying the door handle.

At the elevators, Kaltenborn firmly pushes the button. "Where were you thinking of going now?" he asks Howard.

"Well, my fiancee, Miss Sleep, is still burning." Howard shakes his head in disgust. "Uhh—Miss Burns is still sleeping. And I thought—maybe I could just sit in the lobby and wait until she gets up?" Howard asks cautiously.

Kaltenborn shakes his head. An elevator arrives and Howard steps in.

"Well, I'm really sorry about the room," Howard says.

"Oh, that's all right. We have lots of others," Mr.

Kaltenborn says. The elevator door closes. Kaltenborn looks sadly at the door handle in his hand, turns and goes back down the corridor to wait for the janitors.

In the elevator, Howard presses the button for the lobby, and watches as the floor indicator panel shows that the elevator is going up. He wonders why that should surprise him at all. Resigned, he leans against the back of the elevator, and when it stops he steps out.

He finds himself on the roof of the hotel, which is in the process of being remodeled into a restaurant. Glass walls enclose the roof, and in the early morning light San Francisco is spread before him in panoramic splendor. Howard glances around the room, then turns to reenter the elevator. The door closes in his face. He rings the button, and steps further into the room, heading for the far glass wall to get a better look at the skyline of the city until the elevator reappears.

He weaves his way across the canvas covered floor, past tables and chairs and unidentifiable objects, all of which are covered with paint-spattered drop cloths, past ladders and buckets of paints, which he carefully avoids. In the far distance, the outline of the Golden Gate Bridge is marked with lights; on the street below, cars are small and toylike. The city is beginning to wake up.

The elevator bell rings, and slowly Howard returns across the floor toward the elevator. As he reaches it, the door closes and it begins to descend. He pushes the button once again, and wanders about the room. He puts his overnight case down and leans, tired, against a large object in the center of the room, covered with a drop cloth. The shape is familiar.

Howard lifts the corner of the drop cloth. As he had suspected, it is a piano. He exposes the keyboard and absently hits a few notes. Then he looks around. A short distance away is a three-foot high step ladder. He pulls it over to the piano and sits on it, aimlessly beginning to hit notes and chords on the keyboard. He looks at the fingers on his right hand. They are covered with dust from the keys. Howard pulls at the drop cloth over the piano to wipe his hand and the keyboard.

Judy Maxwell wakes up. She had spent the night asleep on the piano under the drop cloth. Smith's overnight case is beside her. She is dressed in her street clothes, and she straightens her skirt as she watches Howard, the beginnings of a smile appearing at the corners of her mouth. She sits up carefully.

Howard has not looked up and now, the keys cleaned of dust, he begins to play a dirge.

"Of all the gin joints in all the towns in all the world," Judy says, "he walks into mine."

Howard looks at Judy, starts to say something, doesn't, and looks back at the piano. He wonders why he isn't the least bit surprised.

"Play it, Sam," Judy says throatily, getting up and off the piano to come stand by Howard.

"I don't . . . ."

"*You must remember this,*" Judy interrupts, singing. Quickly she moves behind Howard. She puts his finger on the lead note in the treble and reaches around him to hit the bass chord with her left hand.

"*A kiss is still a kiss, a sigh is just a sigh . . . .*"

Howard looks at her over his shoulder, bewildered.

"Keep going, keep going," Judy says. "*The fundamental things apply, as time goes by.*"

"You're very . . . talented," Howard tells her.

"Thanks." She continues the song. "*And when two lovers woo, they still say. . . .*" Judy holds the chord, looks at Howard and digs him with her elbow. "*They still say. . . ."* She sings the line again, leaning closer to Howard. He gets the point.

"I love you," he whispers.

"*I love you,*" she sings. "*On that you can rely, no matter what the future brings . . .*"

Judy leans over now for a kiss, but Howard edges away. The ladder collapses, and they both fall onto the floor. Judy laughs, amused. Howard does not.

"What's the matter?" Judy asks.

"The future," Howard says glumly, cautiously moving his arms and legs to check out the possible damage.

"What's the matter with the future?" Judy asks.

"Well, judging from the recent past . . ." He leaves the sentence dangling.

"Listen," Judy says. "You know what Edmund Burke said? 'You can never plan the future by the past.'"

Howard looks at her oddly. "I beg your pardon," he says.

"I guess you're wondering what a nice girl like me is doing quoting an eighteenth century guy like Edmund Burke, huh?" she asks.

"Yes." Howard stretches out his legs and leans back on his hands, relieved to find nothing broken.

"I was a political science major at Colorado State," Judy explains.

"Is that where you gathered all your information on rocks?" Howard asks, pointing to the overnight case on the floor near the piano.

"Hey, look you've got a case just like mine," Judy says, pointing to the case on the piano top.

"Oh, yes."

"No," Judy says.

"No?" Howard says, confused. He wonders if it is to be a permanent condition.

"No. Advanced geology at Wellesley," Judy tells him.

"What about the music?" Howard asks, pointing to the piano.

"Bennington. Music appreciation."

"And the . . . ."

"Comp Lit, Northwestern," Judy interrupts to explain.

"Is that it?" Howard asks, sitting up and folding his legs beneath him.

Judy shakes her head. "Archaeology, Tuskegee Institute. General semantics at the University of Chicago. Veterinary medicine at Texas A. and M. Say 'when.'"

"What were you trying to become?" Howard asks.

"An alumnus," Judy says wistfully.

"*Alumna.* Feminine," Howard corrects automatically.

"Oh, yeah. That's why I flunked Latin at Goucher."

"Why is it so important to you? Why don't you just stop trying?" Howard asks, puzzled.

"It's important to my father," Judy explains. "He was pretty upset when I was asked to leave the first college I went to."

"Asked to leave?"

"Bounced," Judy confesses, lowering her eyes and toying with a loose thread at the hem of her skirt. "You want to know why?"

"Why?" Howard asks her.

"Oh—nothing really." Judy pulls the thread and grimaces as a section of her hem unravels. "There was this little classroom that burned down," she explains finally.

"Burned down?" Howard waits for Judy to continue.

"Blew up, actually," she tells him, with a gesture of her hand for emphasis.

"Political activism?" he asks.

Judy shakes her head. "Chemistry major," she explains.

"I see," Howard says.

"And then he sent me someplace else and that didn't work out. None of them did," Judy says in a rush. "Some of it was nice. I mean—I read a lot of good books and I went to a lot of movies mostly. But something always seemed to go wrong."

Howard silently shakes his head, understanding what she means. "Where did you come from this time?" he asks after a while.

"Oh—some dumb little college in the Midwest," Judy tells him.

"What happened?"

"Ah—it was silly." Judy looks at Howard, who is watching her with interest. She bites the inside of her lip, then explains. "There was this fellow I liked and he wouldn't pay any attention to me."

"Yes?"

"So I just grabbed him one day in the center of the campus. Actually, I sort of tackled him and gave him a big kiss and he got upset and ran away." Judy looks at Howard hopefully for understanding.

"Well," Howard says sympathetically, "he was probably very shy."

"He was the President of the College," Judy says in a soft voice.

"Yes," Howard agrees. "That would make a difference."

"Anyway," Judy continues, "now I'm kind of scared to go home."

Howard nods. "So am I," he says.

"How do you mean?" Judy asks.

"Well, we—Eunice and I—came all the way from Iowa," Howard explains. "The Conservatory got together this fund so that I could win this grant. But I would say that it doesn't look so good," Howard says glumly.

"Oh my God. I forgot to give you the letter!" Judy jumps to her feet.

"What letter?" Howard asks.

Judy takes an envelope from her pocket and gives it to Howard, then sits again on the drop cloth on the floor, close beside him. The envelope is open.

"That was under your door when I came back to your room last night," Judy explains. She smiles at him broadly.

Howard looks at the torn envelope. "Did you open this?" Howard asks.

"How else could I have read it?" Judy asks reasonably.

Howard takes the letter out of the envelope and looks at it. He sits up slowly as he reads it.

"Did you . . ." he says to Judy, overcome. "Mr. Larrabee says. . . ."

"I know. I saw it," Judy says. "I. . . ."

In a burst of inarticulate enthusiasm, Howard grabs Judy and kisses her.

"It's the grant. The twenty thousand dollars," he says happily.

"I know. I know," Judy says. She pulls him back for another kiss.

Howard finally breaks free and comes up for air. "I've got to tell Eunice," he says.

"Of course you do," Judy agrees. She pulls him back for another kiss.

"After all, she is my. . . ." Howard breaks off the sentence, grins at Judy and kisses her again. Suddenly he breaks off the embrace. "Eunice is my fiancee," he says firmly.

"Of course she is," Judy agrees.

They kiss.

"She deserves to be the first. . . ." Judy puts a finger to Howard's lips, silencing him, and leans over to kiss him.

"Or at least the second," he continues, momentarily breaking away.

Judy throws her arms around Howard's neck, and slowly he returns the embrace, pulling her close.

"Where was I?" Howard asks.

"Eunice," Judy says.

"Who's Eunice?" he asks, lying back on the drop cloth on the floor, and pulling Judy with him.

The elevator bell rings.

A painter in a white, paint-spattered overall outfit and cap, carrying a long ladder under one arm and holding a can of paint with an open top in his other hand, enters the roof room from the elevator. A half smoked cigar dangles from his mouth. He stops in the doorway suddenly and stares into the room. He remains stock-still for a long moment, and then slowly opens his mouth. The cigar falls into his bucket of paint. He shuts his eyes and backs out of the room, turns around, knocking over a lamp on a table, and retreats back into the elevator.

In the hotel lobby, Fritz is talking on the phone to a man he only knows as Big Jim, making arrangements for the delivery of Mrs. Van Hoskins' jewelry. Harry is sitting in his easy chair in the lobby, reading a newspaper.

"Tom, Dick and Horatio?" Fritz says. "They will meet my man at that address? All right. It is set then," Fritz says. He hangs up the phone, satisfied.

In room 1713, Smith has fallen asleep. The ashtray on the table beside him is filled. The overnight case is at his feet. He has loosened his tie, and he needs a shave. It is a restless sleep. He shifts his position in the chair, and his head turns to the other side. He snores softly.

In room 1715, Mrs. Van Hoskins has awakened. She lies in bed, propped against her pillows. Soon she will call William to make plans to use his limousine for the day. She contemplates the shopping possibilities, quite satisfied with the day's prospects.

Outside the hotel, Jones is walking past the main entrance. He has now circled the hotel four times, while running over a plan of action in his head. The golf bag is over his shoulder. He feels his chin ruefully; he badly needs a shave. At the far corner is a coffee shop. He decides to have a quick breakfast before returning to the 17th floor of the hotel and attempting to retrieve the overnight case with the documents.

Howard, carrying the Van Hoskins overnight case, has taken the elevator down to the 17th floor and now knocks on the door to room 1714. "Eunice, please open the door for a minute," he says. "I have some wonderful news." He knocks again, louder.

The door opens a few inches. Eunice's sleep mask is pushed up on her forehead. She does not look good. She is wearing her bathrobe, which is half burned away.

Howard is taken aback at Eunice's appearance. He steels himself and smiles pleasantly.

"I do not want your apologies, Howard," Eunice says. "I think it is too late for that."

"All right, Eunice."

"Have you no heart!" Eunice shrieks.

Smith, in the room across the hall, starts awake at the sound of Eunice's voice, stands immediately and picks up the overnight case. He relaxes a bit, puts the case down and reaches for a cigarette.

"I would think that after what you have done to

me, you would come crawling for forgiveness," Eunice is telling Howard in a shrill voice. "But crawling cannot erase the injustices that have been visited upon me in this horrible place." Eunice turns her back on Howard, crossing her arms on her chest.

"I want you to hear this letter," Howard tells her. "Listen. 'Dear Howard.' Did you hear that? 'Howard.'"

"It is your name," Eunice says.

Howard reads her the letter. "'The Committee and I are agreed that barring any unforeseen circumstances, you will be the next recipient of the Larrabee grant.'"

Eunice has relented a bit, and turned around to face Howard, opening the door a little further. Howard still stands in the corridor.

"'Please join me and my guests,'" Howard continues reading from the letter, "'for luncheon at my home around noon and don't forget to bring your charming fiancée.' Signed, Frederick. 'Frederick Larrabee, Eight-eight-eight Russian Hill.' Look, Eunice, he signed it Frederick. Howard—and Frederick." Howard holds out the letter to Eunice to show her. She turns away. "Uh—'P.S. Perhaps you might favor us with a demonstration of your prehistoric rhythms. F.' See—Frederick here—and down here—F."

"I fail to understand how he can refer to me as your charming fiancée when he has never had the pleasure of meeting me," Eunice points out, angry again.

"Eunice, we can straighten all that out this afternoon," Howard assures her.

Eunice stares at him, her mouth set in a disagreeable thin line. "All right, Howard," Eunice says finally. "Although I no longer have the—trust—I had in you previously, I still have great respect for your work." She reaches up, removes the sleep mask from

100

her forehead, and pats at her hair. "It will take me some time to get dressed," Eunice continues. "You go ahead without me, and I will follow as soon as I can. The address again, please?" she asks.

Howard checks the letter in his hand. "Uh—Eight-eight-eight Russian Hill," he reads off to her. "Try to be. . . ."

Eunice closes the door firmly, shutting off Howard's sentence. He stands outside the door, then reaches down for the overnight case at his feet.

The door to room 1713 is open a crack, and Smith is looking out. He watches Howard. His eyes have widened as he notices the overnight case that Howard picks up and carries with him as he moves down the hall. Smith's eyes follow the case. When Howard enters the elevator, Smith closes the door to his room, rushes over to the case he has put on the bureau, and opens it. He looks inside, and angrily pulls out a handful of clothes and a long white pleated nightgown. He slams them back into the case, slams it shut and stands looking at it, gritting his teeth. "Eight-eight-eight Russian Hill," Smith mutters to himself.

In the lobby, Fritz and Harry stand on one side of a large white pillar, talking softly. Harry is carrying a laundry bag with Howard's case in it, which he has retrieved from the basement utility room.

"It is all set with Big Jim," Fritz says. "Take the case to four-five-nine Dirella Street," he tells Harry. "Deliver it to the boys on the second floor. Tom, Dick and Horatio."

"Four-five-nine Dirella Street," Harry repeats, "Tom Dick and Horatio. Roger."

"Fritz."

Harry crosses the lobby to the escalators and goes down. Fritz goes to the front desk and starts to busy himself with hotel chores that need to be attended.

Judy, Smith's case in her lap, sits in a chair in the lobby behind the large white pillar. She has eavesdropped on Fritz's conversation with Harry, and now peeks out from behind the pillar to watch Fritz. "Four-five-nine Dirella Street," she says to herself. Howard exits from the elevator and crosses the lobby. Judy waves to him.

"Well," Howard tells her, "it's all set. Eunice is going to get dressed and meet us there. I think its really going to work," he says.

"Sure," Judy says. "What can go wrong?"

"Please," Howard cautions. "Don't you say that!"

Judy stands up and puts a hand on Howard's arm to reassure him. "You'll just tell Larrabee that Eunice is really Eunice and that the Eunice he thinks is Eunice isn't Eunice," she explains.

"Right," Howard agrees. "And what will you say?"

"About what?" Judy asks.

"About yourself."

"Oh—I'll just say I'm a girl you picked up in a drugstore and . . . ."

"No, no," Howard interrupts quickly, shaking his head firmly. "You don't say that. You don't say anything," he tells her.

"Right," Judy agrees. "I don't say anything. I just sit there and nod."

"Yes," Howard says. "And then this whole terrible episode will be over."

Judy reaches up and straightens Howard's bow tie gently. "And what about us?" she asks softly.

"And us—we'll say—good-bye." Howard nods, reassuring himself.

Judy looks at him skeptically.

"It's that simple," Howard says firmly. He ponders a moment. "I think," he adds.

"Okay," Judy says, moving away a little bit. "You go get a taxi. I'll be out in a minute," she says.

"All right." Howard goes toward the lobby door, carrying the overnight case.

Judy waits until Howard is outside the hotel, then quickly moves to the corridor to the left of the front desk. She picks up a house phone.

"Room seventeen fourteen," she says. "Miss Eunice Burns, please."

Judy turns to the phone and holds her nose. "Miss Burns?" she says in a Brooklyn accent.

Eunice is putting on her shoes while talking into the phone. "Yes?"

"This is Sylvia, Mr. Larrabee's personal secretary. I am afraid there's been a mix-up in the invitations for this afternoon's luncheon," Judy says apologetically.

"Yes?" Eunice says.

"The luncheon has been switched from Mr. Larrabee's home to one of the Larrabee Foundation offices."

"Oh? Well, Dr. Bannister has already . . . ."

"Yes," Judy quickly tells Eunice. "The desk clerk managed to catch Dr. Bannister before he left the hotel. The address of the luncheon is—do you have a pencil, darling?—uh—four-five-nine Dirella Street," Judy says.

"Dirella?" Eunice repeats.

"Yes. Second floor."

"I see," Eunice says. "Well, thank you, Miss. . . . ?"

"Louise," Judy says.

"I thought you said Sylvia."

"Yes. Sylvia-Louise. With a hyphen. Good-bye." Judy hangs up, and overnight case in hand, she crosses the lobby and heads for the door where Howard is waiting with a cab.

Standing behind the desk, Fritz watches Judy cross

the lobby, a slightly puzzled expression on his face as he notices her overnight bag. With a shrug he returns to his work.

Smith comes out of the elevator, carrying Judy's overnight case. He sees Judy walking out the door, notices her case, pauses for a moment at the elevator, and then quickly crosses the lobby to the front door.

As Smith passes the main desk, Fritz looks up and then straightens, a hand going to his chin and rubbing it as he sees the overnight case in Smith's hand. As Smith goes to the door and out through it, Fritz moves around from behind the desk, crosses the lobby purposely and peers out the front door of the hotel.

Howard is holding a cab door open. Judy gets in, carrying her case, then Howard, carrying his.

Smith is opening the door to the taxi next in line, and now enters the back seat, taking Judy's overnight case in with him. The cab pulls away, after the one with Howard and Judy.

Jones, standing behind a tree a short way down the street, now hurries off the sidewalk and hails a cab going in the other direction. He gets in, lugging his golf bag behind him. The cab makes a U-turn and follows Smith's taxi.

Fritz, still standing in the hotel doorway, has watched the procession with puzzled interest. A frown creases his forehead, and there is an uneasy feeling in his stomach. He stands aside to let a guest enter the hotel, and walks slowly back toward the main desk just as a loud shriek fills the lobby from the elevator area. Fritz turns to investigate.

Mrs. Van Hoskins, in her hot pants sleeping outfit, is rushing from the elevator area into the lobby, totally distraught.

"I've been robbed!" she screams. "My jewels!" She

collapses to the floor in the middle of the lobby, as people begin to gather around her.

Fritz pushes his way through the crowd that has gathered around Mrs. Van Hoskins and begins to help her up. He is not happy.

CHAPTER EIGHT

Harry steps into the second floor room of the only building in sight on Dirella Street. It is a hideous, ratty room, with a bare light bulb hanging from the ceiling above a small round table in the center of the floor. There are four chairs around the table, and three large men in the room. One stands by the wall, where a window might be expected, but there are no windows in the room. Bearing a slight resemblance to an ape, the man standing by the wall is wearing gray slacks and a gray shirt, with a white on white tie. His arms hang loosely by his sides.

The man sitting by the table has short blond hair. He is smoking a cigar, and toying with a large tie tack on his wide, striped tie. He is wearing a black suit, white shoes, and a scowl on his face.

"I'm Tom," the man who opened the door says. He towers over Harry, who is carrying the laundry bag with the overnight case. There is a scar down the side of Tom's cheek. He is wearing a purple sports jacket with his black slacks.

"That's Dick," Tom says, pointing to the man sitting at the table. "That's Horatio." Tom gestures with his head to the man standing near the wall.

Harry walks to the table and spills the overnight

case out of the laundry bag. The three thugs look at it expectantly.

Judy and Howard ride silently in the back seat of the taxi to Larrabee's house. They look out of different sides of the cab. Smith's taxi is close behind, and the one carrying Jones follows Smith's, separated by two cars. On Russian Hill, the cab conveying Judy and Howard slows down to check the house addresses, then pulls to the curb. Smith's cab pulls in behind, and Jones' stops further down the street. Howard and Judy leave their taxi and climb the steps to Larrabee's house. Howard rings the bell. Their cab pulls away. Smith, keeping an eye on Judy and Howard, gets out of his cab with Judy's overnight case. Further down the street, lugging his golf bag, Jones pays his taxi driver and moves behind a tree, keeping Smith in sight.

In a thoroughly rotten section of town, by the waterfront, Eunice is standing by a cab, paying the driver. She looks around in dismay. "You're sure this is the right address?" she asks the driver. The house stands alone at the end of the wharf.

"Four-five-nine Dirella Street, lady," the driver says. "You don't want me to wait, do you?" he asks.

"Yes, I do," Eunice says.

"I didn't think so," the driver says, pulls his head back into the cab and drives off down the street. Eunice watches him go with a perplexed look, then she approaches the building.

Eunice climbs the creaking outside staircase to the second floor. She listens at the only door and hears voices from inside the room. She knocks. There is no answer. The voices stop. Eunice pushes the door open and steps inside the room.

Tom and Dick are standing by the table in the center of the room. Harry is sitting in a chair, and

107

Horatio's hands are around Harry's neck. On the table, Howard's overnight case is open, and several of his igneous rock tambula drums are on the table. Harry looks very frightened.

"This can't be the Larrabee. . . ." Eunice stops as she sees the overnight case and Howard's drums. She walks boldly into the room.

"Why," Eunice says, "Those are Howard's. What on earth are you doing with Howard Bannister's rocks?"

With a sigh of relief Harry sinks into the chair as Horatio releases his neck. Tom, Dick and Horatio have all started heading for Eunice, who begins slowly to back away from the table.

Tom shuts the door. Eunice leans against it and smiles feebly at the glowering thugs.

The door to the Larrabee house is held open by a servant. Larrabee comes forward to greet Howard and Judy at the door. "There they are!" he says warmly. "Our two stars. Congratulations, Howard." Larrabee shakes Howard's hand.

"Thank you, Mr. Larrabee," Howard says.

"Frederick," Larrabee says.

"Frederick," Howard repeats. "And now I'd like you to know something."

Larrabee takes Judy's arm and leads her through the hall into the large, airy living room, where a group of well dressed, interesting looking people are assembled.

"I want you to come in here, Burnsy, and meet my friends," Larrabee tells Judy.

"Wait!" Howard has been left behind at the front door. "Wait a minute. . . ."

The servant who opened the door has politely blocked Howard's way. "May I take that, sir?" The servant asks, reaching for the overnight case.

"No, no I'll keep it, thank you," Howard tells him,

his eyes on Judy, who is now in the center of the living room with Larrabee.

Simon appears in the hallway and smirks at Howard's formal clothes. "I see you're dressed for a celebration," Simon says. "What happened, Bollister? Did your other clothes—burn up?" he says nastily.

"Bannister," Howard says, but Simon has turned and purposely walked into the living room. Howard follows.

Larrabee is introducing Judy to his friends. Simon comes up beside them, and Howard comes up behind him.

"And, of course, you remember our Mr. Simon," Larrabee says to Judy.

"Ahh, Miss—Burns, isn't it," Simon says.

"No," Judy says.

Simon is taken aback, the wind out of his sails. Larrabee looks at Judy. Howard gulps, ready to start his difficult explanation.

"It's—Burnsy," Judy says.

"Of course, of course," Larrabee says.

"Ladies and gentlemen and Mr. Larrabee," Howard begins.

"Frederick," Larrabee reminds him.

"Mr. Frederick," Howard continues. "The fact is— that is to say—what I'm trying to point out . . . ."

"What Howard's trying to say," Judy breaks in, "is how much he appreciates your wonderful hospitality and how many times we'll think of you when we're back in good old Iowa." Judy smiles at the room at large.

Howard groans.

"What compelling sentiments," Simon says.

Judy takes Simon's arm and leads him aside. "Did anyone ever tell you that you were very very sexy?" she asks him quietly.

109

"Well—actually—no," Simon admits, nonplused.

"They—never—will," Judy tells him.

Simon glares at her angrily. "I myself have a little announcement to make that may be of some interest," Simon says, still glowering at Judy. "My natural curiosity led me to do some research on Mr. Bunkester and *Miss Burns*, and I think . . . ."

"I think it can wait until after we've heard Howard give us a little recital on those famous rocks of his," Larrabee interrupts. "How about it, Howard?" Larrabee asks.

Larrabee's suggestion is seconded by the other guests in the room, who applaud politely. Howard agrees. Simon moves away, snarling slightly. Judy eyes Simon anxiously.

While Howard looks around the room for a suitable place, Larrabee makes an explanation to his guests.

"For those of you who are unfamiliar with Dr. Bannister's theory of prehistorical rhythmical and percussive communication," Larrabee begins, "let me point out that the para-notational code in the Tassili rock paintings gives a clue. . . ."

In the dingy room on Dirella Street, Tom is repacking Howard's rocks into the overnight case. Dick has taken Harry with him, and they have gone to fetch Big Jim's limousine from the garage down the street. Horatio is standing behind Eunice, who sits at the table.

"Be careful with that rock, you thug," Eunice tells Tom, who has thrown the last of the igneous formations into the case.

"Shut up, lady," Tom tells her.

"I will not," Eunice cries defiantly.

"Shut her up," Tom tells Horatio.

Horatio lifts Eunice from the chair as if she were a feather, turns her around to face him, and taps her

110

lightly on the cheek, drawing himself up to his full six feet five.

Eunice shuts up.

In the Larrabee living room, Howard is sitting down in the middle of the floor, facing the guests who have arranged themselves in a semi-circle around him. Howard has the overnight case he carried into the house on his lap, the lid open, and he is staring down into it catatonically.

Judy comes over to him and bends down. "What's the matter, Howard?" she asks. "Howard!"

"I think . . . I think. . . ."

Judy leans over and glances down into the overnight case on his lap. It is filled with Mrs. Van Hoskins' jewelry. They both are speechless, staring into the case.

Larrabee, who is sitting opposite Howard, is getting a bit impatient. "Is something the matter?" Larrabee asks.

"Wrong case," Howard says. He slams it shut. Larrabee looks around the room, notices Judy's case, which she had placed on the floor beneath a table at the entrance to the living room, and he gets up to bring the case to Howard.

"Identical traveling cases," Larrabee points out to his friends. "Sweet, isn't it?" Larrabee looks down at Howard and Judy, sitting on the floor, and beams at them affectionately. He hands Judy the second overnight case and resumes his seat.

Judy slowly takes the overnight case of jewelry from Howard's lap, opens it for another peek, then gives Howard the case she had brought with her. Both of them stare nervously as Howard slowly opens the second case. It is full of folders. They stare at the Top Secret stamp on the face of the folder on top.

Slowly, Howard closes the case. "I think a slight error has been made somewhere," he says calmly.

Simon takes the cue and jumps up to face Larrabee and the guests. "The slight error, mesdames and messieurs," Simon says, "is in the so-called identity of these alleged colleagues." Simon pulls himself up on his heels, a triumphant smile on his face. "I don't know who *he* is," Simon says, pointing to Howard. "But *she* is definitely not herself." Simon turns dramatically to point a finger at Judy.

"What are you babbling about, Simon?" Larrabee asks.

"*Nobody move.*"

Smith stands just inside the door to the living room, looking very nervous. His hand is in his jacket pocket as though holding a gun. Everyone freezes.

"I want that case," Smith says, putting the overnight case he is carrying down on the floor.

"Which one?" Howard asks.

"What? Don't confuse me," Smith says.

"Careful," Larrabee cautions. "He may have a loaded gun in his pocket."

"Or an unloaded hand," Judy points out.

"Don't test me," Smith warns. He takes a single step into the room. "Just give me the case," he says.

"*Which one?*" Howard asks again.

"*Either one!*" Smith tells him. "Just slide one over here," Smith directs, aiming his pocket at Howard. Howard slides one of the cases across the marble floor to Smith, who kneels down and starts to open it.

"*Don't move!*"

Coming from the balcony into Larrabee's living room is Jones. He has a gun in one hand and the golf bag in the other.

Smith and Jones eye each other warily across the room. Cautiously Smith gets up, removing his hand

112

slowly from his pocket, and holding it up to show Jones it is empty.

"Get away from that case," Jones tells Smith.

Smith backs off carefully.

"This is inexcusable," Larrabee says in a huff, getting to his feet. "You can't come in here uninvited." He looks at his guests for support. Several of the women faint.

Jones ignores Larrabee, climbing down from the balcony and coming forward into the room. Larrabee begins to move toward Jones.

"Stand back, all of you," Jones says. "All I want is that case." He looks at the second case. "Or that one," he says, confused. Then he notices the third case. "Or maybe that one," Jones says.

Jones cautiously circles the room and heads for the case Smith had with him when he entered the living room. Jones kneels down before it, throwing the golf bag into a corner. He fumbles with the case with one hand while he covers the people in the room with the gun in his other hand.

"Howard!"

From the side entrance to the living room, Eunice enters. She is being pushed into the room by Horatio. Tom is behind her, and Dick behind him. Tom, Dick and Horatio are all carrying guns. Tom is carrying Howard's overnight case.

"Howard," Eunice calls, "they have your rocks!" She points to the overnight case Tom is carrying.

Several more women and one man faint at the sight of the hoods and their guns.

"Don't nobody do nothing," Horatio warns the people in the living room.

"This is unheard of!" Larrabee protests.

Simon falls to his knees. "For God's sake, don't shoot me," he pleads. "I'm part Italian."

113

Larrabee looks at Simon with disgust.

Tom steps forward and puts Howard's overnight case down on the floor, then he steps around Eunice and heads across the room to the case near Smith.

Dick, aiming his gun at Larrabee, moves over to the case near Jones. Jones has his hands in the air. Dick takes Jones' gun away from him, unloads it and tosses it in the corner next to the golf bag.

Horatio kicks Howard's case out of his way and moves toward Judy in the center of the room and the overnight case on the floor next to her.

"Don't you dare kick those priceless rock samples, you Philistine!" Eunice shrieks, hitting at Horatio's back with flailing arms.

Horatio stops and turns around slowly, raising his hand to strike Eunice.

Larrabee quickly moves across the room, and pushes Eunice behind him to protect her. "Don't you dare strike that brave, unbalanced woman!" Larrabee says angrily.

Horatio brings back an arm to hit Larrabee, and Larrabee leaps at him, bouncing off like a basketball. Horatio, knocked off balance, falls onto the couch into the laps of several guests.

Simultaneously, Jones jumps Dick and Smith tackles Tom. Tom's gun is jarred loose from his hand and glides across the marble floor, coming to rest near the couch.

Howard drops to his hands and knees and crawls along the living room floor after the overnight case with his igneous rock drums, which has skittered to the far wall. Judy jumps up from the floor and joins the fray.

Horatio has managed to extricate himself from the guests on the couch and now moves menacingly toward Larrabee. Larrabee, joined by Eunice, tackles

Horatio and brings him to the floor. Eunice begins hitting Horatio on the head with her pocketbook.

By the door to the living room, Jones and Dick, Smith and Tom are having a free for all, grappling for Dick's gun and kicking the overnight cases around when they get in the way. The cases slide easily across the marble floor and disperse around the room.

Judy picks up a bowl of cheese dip from a table and moves with it to the door, where she shoves it in Dick's face. Jones gives her a nod of thanks, and moves to help Smith with Tom.

The servant who had opened the door for Howard and Judy comes into the living room to investigate.

Eunice is now sitting on Horatio's chest, holding onto his tie. Horatio's gun goes off, hitting a light bulb in the chandelier.

The servant walks back out of the living room.

Simon tries to crawl under a chair, and when that fails he seeks refuge under a table.

Near the door, Dick has jumped on Jones' back, pulling him off Tom, who has Smith in an armlock. Jones reaches back and pokes Dick hard in the stomach. Dick's gun flies out of his hand, and skitters across the marble floor. Judy grabs Dick by the hair, and pulls.

Howard, who had almost reached his overnight case, sits back on his heels in dismay. One of the guests has kicked the case, and it moves to the other side of the room, near two of the other overnight cases.

"My Pre-Jurassic Tambula percussion relics!" Howard moans, sticking out a foot and tripping Horatio, who had freed himself from Larrabee and Eunice and is heading to help Tom and Dick near the door.

A uniformed maid picks up the loose gun near the

couch and begins firing wildly into the air. Larrabee runs across the room and subdues her.

Judy suddenly retreats from the fight at the door, and heads for Howard. "Hi," she says. "Having fun?"

"I can't find my rocks!" Howard says.

"Let's grab the cases," Judy says.

"Which one?" Howard yells.

"All of them!" Judy yells.

Judy crawls to two of the cases and picks them up. Howard scuttles across the room and grabs the other two cases and they run out of the living room.

Jones has Dick on the floor near Tom, who is battling with Smith. Horatio is busy freeing himself from Eunice, who is desperately clutching onto one of his legs, and Larrabee, who is holding onto the other.

The servant politely opens the front door as Judy and Howard race through the hall with the overnight cases. He closes the door behind them.

Parked a short distance down the street from the Larrabee house is a black nine-passenger limousine. Behind the wheel is Harry. As Howard and Judy run out of the house with the cases, Harry starts pressing wildly on the limousine's horn.

Near the curb, in front of the house, is a grocery boy's delivery bicycle cart. The lid of the cart is open. Howard runs down the stairs, and out into the street.

"Wait a minute," Judy yells. "In here, stick them in here."

The delivery boy, carrying two huge boxes of groceries, is at the top of the stairs approaching the door of a nearby house. He turns around to watch.

Judy has run to the delivery cart and thrown her two cases into the bin.

Howard, following her lead, puts the other two cases into the bin and closes the cart's top.

"How are your legs?" Judy asks him.

Howard, confused, looks down at his legs. "My legs?"

"Never mind!" Judy stops him. She leaps onto the saddle of the bicycle cart and starts to pedal. "Push!" she instructs Howard.

Howard pushes the cart into the street as Judy works the pedals. A car coming along the street swerves just in time to avoid them. Judy looks back. The delivery boy is still standing at the top of the stairs, his mouth open, watching Judy and Howard and his bicycle cart.

Harry gets out of the limousine, still pressing on the horn. In the distance there is the sound of sirens. Anxiously, Harry looks at the door of the Larrabee house. Finally, Tom, Dick and Horatio emerge, bringing Eunice, Larrabee and Simon with them. Simon is protesting loudly. Horatio points his gun at Simon, who meekly becomes silent very quickly. They descend the stairs to the street, heading for the limousine. Harry, relieved, gets back behind the wheel.

"Get on!" Judy yells to Howard, indicating the top of the cart. "Hurry! Come on, Steve, you can do it."

"My name is Howard." After a few clumsy attempts, Howard manages to find a perch on top of the front of the cart, facing forward. He looks back over Judy's shoulder as the bicycle cart, with Judy pedaling, gets moving down the street.

Tom, Dick and Horatio are pushing Larrabee, Simon and Eunice into the back seat of the limousine. Smith comes running out of the house, followed closely by Jones. The delivery boy has finally realized that his bicycle cart is being taken, and he now puts down his cartons of groceries and heads for the street.

Judy and Howard are halfway down the street and the hoods' limousine is pulling away from the curb, its tires screeching. A cab turns the corner onto the block

117

and Smith quickly runs into the street and flags it down. As he climbs into the back seat of the cab, Jones tries to get in with him, but Smith is too quick and gets the door shut. Jones curses and shakes his fist at the back of the cab as it pulls away. The delivery boy is standing beside Jones, shaking his fist as his bicycle cart is pedaled out of sight by Judy.

As Smith's cab takes the corner, a Cadillac convertible swerves and screeches to a stop to avoid hitting the cab. The driver is a dapper, elderly man. Jones quickly runs down the street and leaps over the door into the back seat of the convertible. "Follow that cab," Jones yells. "I'm with the government."

The old man doffs his gray hat and grins happily as he guns the Cadillac's motor and takes off after the taxicab. The delivery boy watches the convertible zoom off unhappily.

On the front of the bicycle cart, Howard turns around to see what's happening. The limousine is catching up, the taxi is close behind, and Howard catches a glimpse of Jones in the convertible behind the cab. "Here they come!" Howard yells to Judy.

"Hang on!" Judy yells. Howard grabs on desperately to the cart as Judy makes a sharp turn onto a new street and he nearly loses his balance.

As Howard turns to look in the direction they are now going, his expression changes to one of complete horror. They are on the crest of a gigantic steep hill, which swoops down, seemingly endlessly, to a cross street at the bottom of the decline, and then up again an equally steep hill.

At the bottom of the hill, in the middle of the cross street, is a huge step ladder with its legs spread out for balance about six feet from each other. A man stands on top of the ladder, attaching the loose end of a long, wide cloth banner to a wire that stretches

118

across the street from the top of an old building to one under construction. The banner is emblazoned: KEEP SAN FRANCISCO CLEAN WEEK.

Two workmen in overalls are starting to cross the street to the unfinished building, carrying one of the world's largest panes of glass. They are being very careful, and are looking down at their feet.

"You're in my way," Judy tells Howard. "I can't see anything."

"Oh, no!" Howard yells as they start down the hill.

"What is it?" Judy asks.

"Don't ask!" he tells her, shutting his eyes and grabbing onto the top of the cart with both hands.

They hurtle down the hill.

The hoods and their prisoners in the limousine, followed by Smith in the taxi and Jones in the old man's convertible, come around the corner and start down the hill after Judy and Howard and the overnight cases in the bicycle cart.

The workmen with the pane of glass have moved directly into the path of the oncoming vehicles when they look up the hill, see what's coming at them, and freeze.

The bicycle cart is still ahead. Howard screams and covers his eyes with an arm as Judy steers the delivery cart, which has gathered tremendous speed coming down the hill, between the legs of the ladder, across the intersection, and up the far hill.

As they pass through, the men carrying the huge glass pane start to move back toward the sidewalk. But the limousine is bearing down on that side of the ladder, and the men with the glass race around to the other side of the ladder as the limousine passes on the right, swerving slightly, and then continuing up the hill after the bicycle cart.

The taxi, with Smith in the back seat yelling directions to the driver, steers around the left side of the ladder, just missing it, and causing the men carrying the glass pane to run back to the right side of the ladder to avoid being hit.

The old man, driving the convertible with Jones in the back seat, is steering like a maniac, his face split in a grin from ear to ear.

The men with the pane of glass move frantically from one side to the other of the ladder, not knowing in which direction to find safety.

The man on the ladder looks down from his perch and sees the convertible swerving from side to side as it comes down the hill. He crosses himself and shuts his eyes as it passes straight in between the legs of the ladder, without an inch to spare.

The men with the glass pane carefully lower it down on its edge on the street for a moment and breathe a sigh of relief.

The delivery cart's momentum has carried it nearly to the top of the other hill, with Judy pedaling furiously, but now it is going more and more slowly, the three cars in pursuit almost catching up to it. Finally, the cart's forward motion stops and slowly it begins to roll backward, down the hill. Judy shrugs and stops pedaling. Judy and Howard crane to look in back of them in the direction they are now rolling.

The bicycle cart begins to pick up speed as the first two cars—the hood's limousine and the taxi with Smith in the back seat—pass the cart, brake and make U-turns, crossing each other and almost colliding, just separating in time to make room for the convertible driven by the old man to pass between them.

The man on the ladder is watching, motionless.

The men with the glass pane look back in disbelief.

The delivery cart has picked up speed, and is now hurtling back toward the intersection. Howard is staring, open mouthed, holding onto the top of the cart for dear life. Judy is looking back over her shoulder.

Close behind them come the limousine, the taxi and the convertible, which is weaving from side to side.

The workmen swing the pane of glass around so its edge is toward the oncoming vehicles, offering less of a target.

As the cart gets to the cross street, going at top speed, backwards, it swerves and almost topples over, but with Howard now riding it like a ketch, Judy manages to keep it upright and to turn it onto the side street in a wide arc.

The men with the glass pane back up quickly, so they are now standing on the far sidewalk, in front of the building under construction, beneath the attached end of the banner. They rest the pane of glass on the sidewalk and again relax momentarily.

The limousine swerves around the corner.

The Smith taxi takes the corner, just missing the ladder and almost colliding with the limousine, which Harry had braked in order to make the turn.

The convertible begins the turn too early, and it goes into a long skid, just coming to a stop at the base of the ladder, and barely touching one of its legs with a rear fender. Slowly, as the old man brings the convertible back into pursuit, the ladder begins to wobble. As the convertible finally turns the corner, the ladder collapses. The man at the top of the ladder holds onto the end of the banner that he was attaching to the wire across the street. The ladder falls out from under him. He hangs by the end of the banner for a moment, then it rips loose and, in a long swinging arc, the man, holding the banner end, swings down toward the street, just missing it with his toes. Following through on the swing, the banner takes him across the street and directly through the center of the pane of glass, shattering it into a million pieces. He lands inside the unglassed window space in the unfinished building.

The workmen stare at each other unhappily, then run to the corner, looking after the convertible, which is just disappearing over the crest of another hill.

The delivery cart is going down a new hill. Howard and Judy now have a fairly good lead on the pursuing cars.

Judy turns another corner. They are at the top of yet another hill, and the bicycle cart picks up speed, with Judy pedaling furiously.

"No!" Howard screams. He ducks.

Judy peers around him, and attempts to brake the cart.

Halfway down the hill, a few blocks up from an intersection, moving slowly and with great ceremony, is a Chinese parade, with a marching band, school children dressed in party clothes, and a long, red, elaborate processional dragon being carried along by two ranks of bearers beneath it. The procession is moving slowly and crowds have gathered on either side on the street. The dragon, leading the parade, has its head held high, and its body moves jerkily as it is animated by the men carrying it.

Howard yells at the top of his lungs.

The people in the procession look around and start to run for the sidewalks. The spectators break up into small groups and run for cover.

The delivery cart reaches the tail of the dragon. The people carrying the dragon anxiously lift it up and the delivery cart passes between the two rows of dragon carriers. When the cart gets to the dragon's head, it tears the entire dragon loose from the bearers, who stand in dismay yelling angrily as their dragon leaves them behind on the street.

The cart is now buried in the head of the Chinese dragon and the entire dragon is zipping down the hill like a monster on the loose.

People stare at it in terror as it goes racing by.

A Chinese mother runs out and picks her child up out of the middle of the street just in time to whisk it out of the path of the oncoming monster.

"Where are we?" Judy asks. "I can't see anything."

"Well, there's not much to see actually," Howard says. "We're inside a Chinese dragon."

"Oh," Judy says.

The dragon reaches the intersection with the cross street at the bottom of the hill, causing a pile up of traffic in both directions, turns a corner and begins to slow down on a level street.

"Look out, Judy!" Howard yells. "Where are you going?"

"I don't know. I can't see."

Howard is kneeling on the front of the cart beneath the dragon's head, peering out one of the eyes. "Watch out!" he yells to Judy.

Judy turns the bicycle's handle and the dragon swerves to avoid a garbage truck, parked at an angle to the curb and blocking half the street. The cart misses the truck, but the tail of the dragon smashes through a large collection of empty garbage cans that are standing beside the truck. As the bicycle cart and dragon continue down the street, it is followed by a half dozen of the garbage cans rolling noisily after it.

A man is crossing the street. He looks up, and stops dead in his tracks. Howard screams at Judy. At the last minute, the dragon swerves to one side suddenly to avoid colliding with the pedestrian and heads into the open door of a store with a sign: COSTUMES

FOR ALL OCCASIONS. Head first, the entire dragon disappears into the store. The garbage cans zoom down the street in its wake.

The man on the street tears his eyes away from the tail of the dragon, now inside the store, and looks back down the street just in time to see the garbage cans bearing down on him. He runs to the nearest sidewalk and leaps head first over a railing as the cans thunder by. The man lands in a below-the-street open-air restaurant, smack on top of a large table loaded with food at which a group of tourists are eating. The table collapses under his weight, and the tourists follow it to the ground.

In the limousine, Larrabee has his arm around Eunice, and she is leaning against his shoulder. Simon is cowering in a corner of the back seat, his hands covering his eyes. Tom, Dick and Horatio are yelling directions at Harry, who is screaming back at them. They have momentarily lost sight of Judy and Howard and the bicycle cart, and now screech to a stop in front of a group of Chinese men on the sidewalk to ask directions. As a group, the men point down the hill, and the limousine takes off again.

The taxi driver, his face grim, nods silently at Smith, who has climbed over the seat into the front of the taxi, and brakes sharply to avoid running into the back of the limousine, which had stopped momentarily on the hill. The limousine starts off, with a squeal of tires, and the cab takes off after it.

The old man driving the convertible now catches up to the back of the taxi, nudging it a bit, and then accelerates to keep on its tail as the taxi picks up speed down the hill following the limousine. In the back seat of the convertible, his face white, Jones sits absolutely motionless. He is holding on tightly to the window frames on either side of the seat. The old man takes his hands off the wheel to wave grandly to a group of bystanders on the sidewalk. Jones slowly closes his eyes and once again holds his breath.

The back door of the costume shop leads to an alley and now, cautiously, Judy and Howard, dressed in oriental robes and hats, carrying the four over-night cases, step out into the alley. As they move quickly away from the door, they hear a car approach. The hoods' limousine turns into the alley a block away, heading toward them.

Quickly Judy and Howard turn in the other direction and begin to run.

"There they are!" Tom yells. Harry accelerates down the alley.

The taxicab turns into the alley, and speeds up after the limousine.

The old man negotiates the convertible into the alley, and follows the cab.

A police car has joined the chase, and follows the convertible.

Judy and Howard turn a corner at the end of the alley, and find themselves on a street in front of a church where a wedding has just been completed. The bride and groom are standing at the top of the church steps, waving to friends and relatives at the bottom of the steps who are throwing rice and confetti. A Volkswagen, with its motor running, is waiting for the newlyweds on the street outside. A *Just Married* sign is attached to the rear bumper of the car.

Judy heads straight for the Volkswagen. A man is standing by the open door on the driver's side of the car. Judy climbs in from the other side, tosses the overnight cases into the back seat and crawls over to get behind the wheel. Howard follows, throws his overnight cases in the back, and pulls the door shut.

"Thank you," Judy tells the man standing by the

car. She pulls the driver's door shut, and steers the Volkswagen out into the street.

The bridal party comes tearing after the car.

The limousine zooms out of the alley, turns the corner and brakes precariously to a stop to avoid hitting the bride and groom. The taxi turns the corner, swerves to avoid the limousine and stops with its bumper nudging the rear right fender of the hoods' car. The old man turns the Cadillac convertible around the corner and manages to stop it, its right front bumper against the license plate of the taxicab. The cars maneuver about, and resume the chase. The wedding party quickly reassembles in front of the steps of the church. The police car turns the corner and takes off after the cars, radioing headquarters for help.

The Volkswagen is heading down another long hill, where it threads its way between two cable cars that are about to pass each other, then turns a corner.

"What are you doing?" Howard shrieks. "This is a one-way street."

"We're just going one way," Judy explains, and steers the car onto another street. Near the bottom of the hill, dumping its load, is a sand truck. A cement mixer is on the sidewalk, and the workmen are in their path.

"Look out! Look out!" Howard yells, shielding his eyes with his arm.

"I *am* looking out," Judy says. She swerves the car just in time to miss the sand truck, but sand dumps on top of the car.

Howard looks behind them, then yells at Judy. "What are you doing?" he shrieks.

"Driving," Judy says. "And for the *first time*," she adds proudly.

"What!" Howard yells with a groan.

"It's a cinch," Judy says, taking her eyes off the road to look at Howard. "Now, what does *this* thing do?" she asks, pointing to the gear shift.

"Let me do it, for Pete's sake."

"Who's Pete?" Judy asks.

Howard slides under Judy and they switch places behind the wheel. Between them and the four cases, the Volkswagen is jammed.

"How are we doing?" Howard asks.

"Here they come," Judy tells him. The hoods' limousine followed by the yellow cab and the Cadillac convertible are hurtling down the hill, all covered with sand from the dump truck.

"You'd better turn," Judy says. "Turn!"

"I'm turning."

Just past the corner is a haulaway truck loaded with Volkswagens, the top back space empty.

"Oh, look at that," Judy yells. "Go up there."

"What?" Howard says, then he sees the haulaway. "No!"

"Yes," Judy insists.

Howard shrugs and drives the Volkswagen up the ramp of the haulaway to the empty space on top. Judy and Howard duck out of sight as the hoods' limousine, followed by the yellow cab and the old man's convertible and a police car turn onto the street and pass the haulaway.

Judy and Howard sit up.

"Now what?" Howard asks.

"Back up," Judy says.

"I knew you'd say that."

The Volkswagen backs down the ramp, makes a U-turn and races off down Van Ness.

Judy looks out the rear window. "I think we lost them," she says with satisfaction. She turns on the radio.

"Good! Could you turn the radio off, please?"

"Oh, sure," Judy says. She turns off the radio, and the windshield wipers go on. Howard looks at her sternly, and she turns off the wipers.

"I think I'd better turn down here, just to be sure," Howard says.

"Good idea," Judy says.

Howard steers the Volkswagen onto Telegraph Place.

A workman is troweling fresh cement in a narrow driveway between two apartment houses. He looks up and jumps out of the way as the Volkswagen drives through the fresh cement and proceeds down the short, steep hill. The street ends in a cross street at the bottom of the hill.

Suddenly the cab carrying Smith appears at the intersection, as the hoods' limousine drives into the alley from the other direction. Howard makes a U-turn and starts back up the hill.

The workman is repairing the damaged cement. He looks up and jumps out of the way as the Volkswagen, the yellow cab, the hoods' limousine, the convertible and two police cars drive up the hill and through the cement, onto a winding road.

"Oh, they're gaining on us," Howard yells, checking in the rear view mirror.

"I think there's a good road right down there," Judy says, pointing.

Howard turns the car, at the intersection of Clay and Pierce, and the Volkswagen, followed by the limousine, the cab, the convertible and the police cars, go hurtling down the long flight of steps to the street at the bottom of the park.

"Okay," Judy yells, "turn here."

Howard shrugs, driving grimly, and makes the turn. "I can't see where we're going," he complains.

"Here, let me clean your glasses for you." She pulls his glasses off.

"Now I really can't see," Howard says. "Judy, I can't see."

"Oh." She puts his glasses back on.

"Oh, God," Howard says, "I can see." He throws his glasses out the window.

Judy is peering out of the back window of the Volkswagen. She ignores Howard, who is watching the road through squinting eyes. "Here they come," Judy yells, spotting the limousine. "Let's go back the other way." Judy reaches over and pushes at the wheel as Howard lets out a yell of protest.

The Volkswagen executes a hairpin turn in the middle of the street, causing complete chaos with the traffic in both directions. A police car turns on its siren.

In the limousine, Larrabee is trying to protect Eunice from Horatio, who is threatening her to be quiet or else. Simon is weeping.

"The other way!" Tom yells at Harry as the Volkswagen zooms past.

Harry brakes and turns the limousine around.

In the taxi, Smith yells at the driver. "Follow them!" he says frantically. The driver swerves around a car and makes a U-turn.

Jones has passed out in the back seat of the convertible. The old man, having a wonderful time, makes the U-turn without being told.

The convertible is now followed by three police cars.

The Volkswagen turns a corner, leaving total confusion on the street in its wake. It is followed closely by the limousine, the taxicab and the convertible and the police cars, sirens blaring.

Howard steers the Volkswagen blindly down a long

hill that ends in the entrance to a ferry. Parallel to the street is a long pedestrian walkway with a canopy over it. Howard uses the blur of color at the corner of his eye to keep the car on the street. He is driving grimly, and Judy is now sitting close to him, helping him steer. He cannot see very well without his glasses.

At the bottom on the hill, a ferry is just about to pull away from its dock. The men who have put up the barriers look back up the hill, see the Volkswagen bearing down on them and run to the side of the street to take cover.

"We can make it!" Judy yells, looking back. The limousine, taxicab and convertible are in close pursuit. The police cars are catching up.

"I can't see! What's down there?" Howard asks desperately.

"We can make it!" Judy repeats.

The ferry pulls away.

The Jones convertible swerves to avoid a cat and jumps the curb at the side of the street, riding down the sidewalk under the canopy.

The Volkswagen hits the bottom of the hill at full speed, and takes off from the dock like a bird.

"I don't think we can make it," Judy says wistfully.

The limousine shoots off the dock after the Volkswagen.

The taxi driver tries to brake the taxi to a stop, but it shoots off the dock after the limousine anyway.

Jones stands up in the back seat of the convertible, jolted awake. His head goes through the canopy and rips it down the middle as the convertible joins the crowd in the water at the end of the dock.

A group of stunned spectators stare in disbelief at the spectacle in the water. The half-dozen police cars that had joined the chase screech to a stop at the water's edge, some of the policemen with drawn guns.

Tom, Dick and Horatio, Harry, the taxi driver and Smith, the old man, Jones, Eunice and Larrabee are all swimming toward the dock. Simon is floundering in the water.

The Volkswagen is floating in the water like a weird water creature. Howard is staring straight ahead, exhausted. Judy rolls up her window and tries gamely to smile at Howard.

"I took life saving at U.C.L.A.," she tells him hopefully.

CHAPTER NINE

In a small, weatherbeaten San Francisco Night Court room, an assorted group of people sit scattered around on the wooden rows of seats facing the front of the court. They are, for the most part, silent. Occasionally the door at the back of the court opens, and a latecomer enters and walks down an aisle to settle into a seat and look anxiously at the empty bench at the front of the court, raised on a platform, that will soon be occupied by the Judge. On the top of the Judge's bench is his gavel. Next to a door in the wall behind and just to one side of the bench, a Bailiff stands with his hands behind him watching the people in the courtroom.

A man in the front row produces a newspaper and begins to read. He turns a page, and the paper rattles loudly. The Bailiff looks at him sternly, and the man sheepishly folds the paper and puts it away.

The door near the Bailiff opens and the Judge, a haggard, nervous man in his sixties, appears and looks out at the courtroom unhappily. He is a tall thin man, and his robes hang loosely on his frame. There is an air of grayness about him.

Slowly the Judge surveys the people in the courtroom, most of whom look away from his glance.

"They're a foul and depraved looking lot, Sergeant," the Judge says quietly to the Bailiff.

"Those are just the spectators, Your Honor," the Bailiff tells him.

"Oh, yes. Of course," the Judge says, looking somewhat relieved. "Well—let's get on with it." The Judge walks purposefully to the raised platform, and begins to step up to take his place behind the bench.

"All stand!" the Bailiff instructs the courtroom in a loud voice.

The Judge starts violently. He turns around to look at the Bailiff with obvious irritation, then turns and climbs onto the platform, catching the hem of his voluminous black magisterial robe on a loose nail at the base of the platform.

The Bailiff addresses the Court, calling it into session, and introducing the Honorable Marvin B. Maxwell as the presiding Judge.

Judge Maxwell is standing on the platform, yanking at his robe to free it from the nail. Finally he gets it loose, but the robe tears. Shaking his head ruefully, the Judge goes to his swivel chair behind the bench and sits down. He looks out at the courtroom.

The spectators are all standing.

The Judge picks up the gavel and brings it down once against the desk. He winces at the noise it makes.

The spectators sit down, and the Judge looks around him expectantly.

The Bailiff now approaches the front of the bench with a sheaf of papers in his hands. The Judge takes them reluctantly, and begins to leaf through them. As he does so, he reaches into a drawer under the bench and brings out several bottles of pills, which he puts on the bench in front of him, along with some pencils and note pads, a roll of Lifesavers and a box of cough drops.

The Bailiff moves to one side, so the Judge can address the courtroom.

The man in the front row shifts position on the hard seat, making it creak loudly in the silent courtroom.

The Judge looks up from his papers, and talks to the spectators in a harsh voice. "Now, I don't want any noise tonight," he says. "No disturbances or demonstrations of any kind. I want peace and calm and order." The Judge sternly surveys the people before him, who shift nervously in their seats. "If there is any nonsense of any kind, I will be merciless," Judge Maxwell continues. "*Merciless.* Is that clearly understood?" The Judge summons the Bailiff, who comes to stand in front of the bench.

"Do you think they understood that, Sergeant?" the Judge asks him.

"Yes, sir, I'm sure they did," the Bailiff assures the Judge.

"All right," the Judge says. "Let's get tonight's horror show on the road."

Suddenly the Judge's face changes color, his hands clench and then he sneezes hugely, sneezes again, and then coughs violently.

"Is Your Honor feeling all right?" the Bailiff asks anxiously.

"No, my honor is not feeling all right," the Judge tells him, getting himself back under control. "My heart is pounding, my metabolism has practically ceased to function and my nerves are completely shot." The Judge wipes his face with his robe, and carefully feels his pulse. He settles back into his swivel chair, his face becoming thoughtful, his eyes closed.

The Bailiff waits for the Judge to continue.

Finally, the Judge sits up and opens his eyes, leaning forward and resting his arms on the bench. "Do you have any idea what it's like to sit here night after night watching this endless stream of human debris floating by?" the Judge asks him.

"Yes, sir, of course I have," the Bailiff answers.

"No, you don't," the Judge says emphatically. "You don't have to decide whether to put them away in some ghastly hellhole or turn them loose so they can commit another hideous offense."

"That's true, sir," the Bailiff says.

The Judge pops a cough drop into his mouth, fingers his chin, and motions the Bailiff to come closer. "I'd like to send every one of them to an island somewhere, wrapped in heavy chains," the Judge confesses. "But you know why I don't, Sergeant?" he continues.

"Why, Judge?" the Bailiff asks.

"Compassion!" The Judge strikes his gavel on the desk for emphasis, causing the Bailiff to move away a bit, and the spectators to start in their seats. The Judge summons the Bailiff closer again.

"I just have too much compassion," the Judge continues, in a softer voice. "And that's why I'm a wreck," he finishes philosophically. He takes a pill from a vial on the bench top. "You know what this yellow pill is for?" he asks the Bailiff.

"What, Judge?" the Bailiff asks.

"To remind me to take this blue pill." The Judge shakes a blue pill from another vial on the desk, and washes them down.

"What's the blue one for, Your Honor?" the Bailiff asks him.

"I don't know," the Judge says sadly. "They're afraid to tell me." He pulls the front of his robe out. "I've lost so much weight in the last year that the only thing that showed up on my X-rays was the wall

135

behind me." The Judge suddenly coughs again, hoarsely.

"Well, Your Honor," the Bailiff says sympathetically when the Judge stops coughing, "I think it'll be pretty quiet tonight."

The Judge nods at the Bailiff with a hopeful expression on his face.

Without warning, and from several directions, the courtroom is assailed by the sound of loud voices and people yelling.

The Judge sits up straight in his chair, grimacing with fear. He looks around the court. The spectators are not responsible.

Through the left detention door comes a police-woman with Eunice and Judy, wrapped in blankets, one of which Judy quickly pulls up over her head as she enters the courtroom. Behind them are two other policewomen, carrying the four overnight cases.

The Judge looks at the women for a moment, then turns to his right at the additional sounds coming from that direction.

Through the door to the men's detention area at the left come three policemen, Howard, Smith, Jones, Tom, Dick and Horatio, Larrabee, Simon, the taxi driver and the old man who was driving Jones in his convertible. They are all also wrapped in blankets.

The Judge sighs in dismay and turns his head away.

Through the front door of the Court now come Mrs. Van Hoskins, wearing a red hot pants outfit, and the delivery boy from whom Howard and Judy stole the bicycle cart. They march boldly down the center aisle to the Judge's bench.

As the groups merge in front of the Judge, he looks down on the scene with horror. Everyone is talking at once, and the noise level is very high. The police-woman with the overnight cases moves to the bench and places them in front of the Judge. With the exception of the police and Judy, who now resembles a mummy, wrapped head to foot in her blankets and standing to one side, everyone is trying to get the attention of the Judge.

Pulling himself together, the Judge picks up his gavel and raps heavily for attention. Slowly the voices subside, and there is quiet in the court.

"All right," the Judge says. "What is the meaning of all this?"

The commotion threatens to begin again, but before it gets out of hand the Judge raps for attention.

"Quiet! Quiet!" he demands. "I will allow each of you who so desires to approach the bench for a one-sentence explanation. Keep that in mind. One sentence. Who wants to be first?"

There is a rush to the front of the Judge's bench, and once again the Judge pounds for order. A crack appears on the top of the desk.

"All right, all right! You," the Judge says, pointing to Howard. "What do you have to say for yourself?"

Howard steps forward. "Your Honor," he says, "all I was trying to do was protect my rocks which were taken by mistake, and if you'll just allow me . . . ."

"No, I won't," the Judge interrupts. "You," the Judge says, pointing to Jones.

"If Your Honor will let me identify myself and the organization that I represent . . . ."

"No," the Judge says. "Not now." The Judge points to Smith.

Smith steps to the front of the bench. "The people have the right to know!" Smith insists. "I have been spied on and persecuted . . . ."

"One sentence!" the Judge yells, pounding with his gavel. "Stand back." The Judge points to Harry.

"A strange guy came up to me on the street," Harry

says in a pleading voice, "and offered me five bucks to deliver . . . ."

The Judge groans and holds his head. "Please don't," he says to Harry. "Next."

Eunice quickly walks to the bench, and in a shrill voice she says, "This is an unspeakable example of man's inhumanity to man."

The Judge peers down at her. "Absolutely correct, madam," he agrees.

Larrabee joins Eunice at the bench. "My home has been invaded by hoodlums, policemen and other un-invited and thoroughly unsavory types, and I . . . ."

"You, Sir, have not been invited," the Judge tells him, motioning Larrabee and Eunice back from the bench. He points to Simon.

Simon walks to the bench, and draws himself up on his heels. "You cannot put a man like myself with a Ph.D. from one of Europe's most eminent universities in such a position," Simon says emphatically.

"Just watch," the Judge tells him. He looks at the rest of the group in front of him. "Okay, you in the purple coat."

Tom straightens his jacket and walks to the bench. "I'm not sayin' nothin' and I'm not pleadin' to nothin' until I get to speak to my lawyer," Tom says.

"Very sensible," the Judge agrees. "You," he says, pointing to Horatio.

"It's a frame-up," Horatio whines. "The gun was planted on me by some business enemy." Horatio steps back and Dick takes his place before the bench.

"This is a case of police brutality pure and simple," Dick says.

"Good," the Judge tells him. "Next." The Judge has his head in his hands now, staring at the people as-sembled before the bench with disbelief.

The taxi driver walks to the bench. "That man over

138

there made me lose a perfectly good taxi," the driver says, pointing to Smith.

The Judge nods at him in sympathy.

"My jewels are in one of those cases," Mrs. Van Hoskins explains, walking to the bench now. "And I demand that they be returned immediately."

"One sentence, lady," the Judge reminds her, waving the Bailiff over to move her away.

The delivery boy comes to the bench. "They stole my delivery bike, Your Honor," the boy says. "That one there and that one there." He points to Howard and to Judy, who is still wrapped in the blankets, making no move to offer an explanation.

The Judge recognizes the old man, who is standing a little behind Larrabee and Eunice, with his hand raised.

"I've got to admit it, Your Honor," the old man says sheepishly, "I've never had so much fun in my life."

"I can't say as that I agree with you," the Judge tells him sadly.

Horatio, who is standing beside Eunice, now accidently takes a step and steps on her foot. Eunice shrieks and hits him on the arm. Immediately everyone is yelling and several fights threaten to break out.

The Judge raps furiously on the bench with his gavel. The crack in the desk widens. He finally stands up and pounds, demanding attention.

"Silence! Silence! *Shut up!*" the Judge yells.

With an effort, the policemen manage to separate Jones and Smith, who have begun to throw punches, and then there is quiet.

"If there are any more outbursts of this nature, I'm going to give somebody orders to shoot to kill," the Judge says. He looks around at the group before him, who now stand quietly, and then glances down at his bench. He picks up the flattened roll of Lifesavers, which he had hit with the gavel, pounding for attention. "You've made me smash my Lifesavers," he says sadly.

The Bailiff reaches in his pocket and hands the Judge a fresh roll of Lifesavers.

The Judge smiles a wan smile of thanks, then looks at the overnight cases on his bench. "Now," he tells the people in the courtroom, "we're going to get this story calmly and clearly. First of all, just what the devil are these?"

"My jewelry," Mrs. Van Hoskins says loudly.

"My rocks," Howard tells the Judge.

"Wait a minute. Wait a minute," the Judge says. "Whom do these cases belong to?" he asks, confused.

"The government!" Jones says, stepping forward.

"The people!" Smith says, stepping in front of Jones.

Jones pushes Smith back out of the way, and two of the policemen quickly come forward and separate them.

"You," the Judge says, pointing to one of the policemen. "What is this all about?"

"There was a robbery, Your Honor," the policeman explains, "and then there was a shooting of some kind in this man's house." The policeman points to Larrabee.

"Thank you, officer," the Judge says. He points to Larrabee. "What is this about a shooting?" the Judge asks.

"I am Frederick Larrabee," Larrabee says, stepping forward.

"I don't care *who* you are," the Judge tells him.

Eunice steps forward indignantly. "He happens to be a *foundation*," she says to the Judge.

"I don't care if he's a pillar of the church," the Judge snaps. "I'm trying to find out about these." The Judge points to the four overnight cases.

140

"I never saw them before in my life!" Horatio says.

"I didn't ask you," the Judge says to Tom.

"I didn't say anything," Dick says.

"I want my bike back," the delivery boy says plaintively.

"I'll give you a bike back," the Judge tells the boy angrily. "I'll give you a broken back if you don't be quiet."

The delivery boy hangs his head unhappily and becomes silent.

The Judge takes a small bottle and a spoon from behind the bench, pours some medicine and drinks it. He turns back to the court and motions the policeman forward again. "Officer. What are these people being charged with?" the Judge asks him.

"That's kind of hard to say, Judge," the policeman tells him.

"Give it a shot," the Judge suggests.

The policeman fingers his chin a moment, then begins to explain. "Well, sir," he says, "we picked some of them out of San Francisco Bay."

"Entering the country illegally?" the Judge asks.

"No, sir, they drove in," the policeman says.

"Into the country?" the Judge asks, leaning forward and leaning his arms on the bench.

"No, sir, into the Bay," the policeman explains.

The Judge begins to make notes. "Okay," he says, "unauthorized use of public waters."

"Mostly in stolen cars," the policeman continues.

"Ahh—that's better," the Judge says, cheering up a bit and rubbing his hands together. "Grand larceny." He makes a note on his pad.

"Then there was the shooting," the policeman tells the Judge.

"That's assault with a deadly weapon." The Judge sits up in his chair.

141

"They broke into my house," Larrabee contributes.

"That's breaking and entering," the Judge says with satisfaction.

Larrabee points to Eunice. "They brought her with them forcibly," he tells the Judge.

"That's kidnapping." The Judge rolls the word around on his tongue.

"They tried to molest me," Eunice tells him angrily.

The Judge looks at Eunice. "That's unbelievable," he says.

Jones steps closer to the bench. Smith tries to join him, but is stopped by a policeman.

"Your Honor," Jones says, "I think I can clear all this up in ten seconds."

"You do and you'll get a prize," the Judge says.

"May I approach the bench?" Jones asks.

"Yes," the Judge says reluctantly. He turns to the Bailiff. "Watch him like a hawk," the Judge instructs.

Jones takes a wallet out of his pocket, extracts some identification papers and hands them to the Judge. "As you can see," Jones says, "I represent our government."

"God bless it!" Horatio says quickly.

"Shut up!" the Judge yells at Horatio. He turns back to Jones. "Go on," the Judge tells him.

Jones turns dramatically to face Smith, pointing him out to the Judge. "I have been following this man's movements for some time," Jones explains. Jones reaches for one of the overnight cases, pushes the latch and prepares to open it. "And, Your Honor," Jones continues, a look of triumph on his face, "I can prove that he is in unauthorized possession of. . . ." Jones pauses dramatically, throws open the case and pulls the top item out with a flourish. "Unauthorized possession of secret government . . . *underwear!*"

142

Jones says in disbelief. "Underwear?" he says to himself, staring at the open top of Judy's overnight case.

"Get the court psychiatrist," the Judge instructs the Bailiff quietly.

Jones has himself back under control, and reaches up to grab another of the overnight cases. The Judge grabs it back.

"Watch out! Those might be my rocks," Howard says loudly.

"Tell him to bring straight jackets," the Judge says to the Bailiff, retrieving the second overnight case from Jones.

"The people have a right to know!" Smith now yells, breaking away from the policeman and heading for Jones.

"In an assortment of sizes!" the Judge tells the Bailiff.

The policeman pulls Smith back, as Jones hastily moves to the far side of Eunice and Larrabee.

"I want my mouthpiece!" Tom yells.

"I demand my civil rights," Dick says.

"I want to decline on the fifth," Horatio adds.

"I never saw these guys before in my life," Harry whines.

The Judge pounds furiously on his bench with the gavel, but the babble before him continues, everyone talking at once.

"There's government property in there!" Jones yells, trying to break away from the policeman holding him to get to the overnight cases.

"All power to the people!" Smith yells back, struggling with the policeman who is holding on firmly to his arm.

"I demand the return of my private property," Mrs. Van Hoskins insists, walking to the bench and trying to retrieve her overnight case. The judge pulls the

case she tries to take away from her, and they strug-
gle.

"I just want my bike back," the delivery boy tells
a spectator in the front row of the court.

Near one side of the group, Eunice has her head on
Larrabee's shoulder. "Frederick, I'm so ashamed," she
says.

"Don't you worry, Eunice," Larrabee assures her,
awkwardly smoothing down her hair.

The Judge has managed to wrestle the overnight
case away from Mrs. Van Hoskins, and now he pounds
furiously with his gavel on the bench, yelling for silence. "Order in the court! Order in the court!" the
Judge yells.

Beside the bench, the Bailiff is also yelling for
order.

The group before the bench slowly settles down.

"Everyone be quiet!" The Judge yells.

"Be quiet!" the Bailiff repeats.

"Silence!" the Judge demands, the courtroom now
being quiet.

"Silence!" echoes the Bailiff.

"You, too," the Judge demands of the Bailiff.

"Me, too!" says the Bailiff.

The Judge looks at the Bailiff angrily, and he becomes silent.

"This is a court of law," the Judge tells everyone in
a stern voice. "*My* court of law. It may not look like
much to you, but it's all I've got. Ordinarily I would
threaten you with contempt." The Judge stops to let
this sink in. "But in this case," he continues, his voice
rising, "and I think the Supreme Court will back me
up on this," he says in an aside to the Bailiff, "I am
seriously considering setting up a *torture chamber*."

The Judge has yelled the end of his sentence, and
now, looking slowly over the people assembled before

him to make certain his message is understood, he wipes his hands on his robe and then sits up straight in his chair.

"Now," the Judge says patiently, "I want this whole ridiculous story told by one person. Anyone think they can handle it?" the Judge asks.

Howard raises his hand.

The Judge examines Howard slowly, and then nods his head. "All right," the Judge says to Howard. He quickly scans the rest of the crowd. "And while he's telling it to me, the rest of you keep whips and hot irons in the back of your minds." The Judge motions Howard to approach the bench.

Howard steps forward. "Well, sir," he begins, "my name is Howard Bannister, and I'm from Ames, Iowa."

"No excuse," the Judge informs Howard.

"No, sir," Howard agrees. "But it all began when I bumped my head in the taxi on the way in from the airport," Howard explains.

"Are you pleading insanity or amnesia?" the Judge asks him.

"Neither," Howard says. "But I went to the drugstore to get something for my headache, and the druggist tried to charge me for a radio because she said her husband would pay for it." Howard points at Judy, wrapped in the blankets. "But I didn't of course," Howard adds quickly.

"Of course," the Judge agrees.

"Anyway," Howard continues, "she ripped my jacket and when Eunice came along . . . ."

"Who's Eunice?" the Judge asks quickly.

Howard points Eunice out to the Judge. "My fiancee," Howard explains.

"You have a wife and a fiancee?" the Judge asks, reaching for his pencil and note pad.

"No, sir," Howard answers. "But when she called me Steve . . . ."

"Your fiancee called you Steve?" the Judge asks Howard, reluctantly putting his pencil down.

"No, sir," Howard says. "My wife. Or, rather, the one who isn't my wife," he corrects.

"What does the one who isn't your fiancee call you," the Judge asks. "Howard?"

"No, sir," Howard says quickly. "The one who isn't my fiancee *doesn't* call me Howard," Howard says positively. "And the one who isn't my wife doesn't call me Howard because the one who isn't my wife is also the one who isn't my fiancee," Howard says reasonably. "The other one who isn't my wife," he continues, "the one who *is* my fiancee, doesn't call me Steve. She calls me Howard. You see?" Howard asks the Judge.

The Judge is taking a pill. "Let's skip over this part and move on," the Judge suggests.

"Yes, sir. Well," Howard says, collecting his thoughts, "that night, at the banquet, she was there again and . . . ."

"Who was there?" the Judge interrupts, trying to clarify the situation. "Your wife or your fiancee?"

"Neither," Howard says.

"You mean there's a third one?" the Judge asks quickly.

"No, sir," Howard tells him. "The one who isn't either. Everyone was calling her Burnsy," he explains.

"Why?" the Judge asks.

"Well, that's short for Burns," Howard explains. "That's Eunice's last name."

"Oh," the Judge says, relieved to finally understand the situation. "So *Eunice* was there," he says.

"No, sir, Burnsy was there," Howard corrects. "Or rather, the one who isn't Burnsy."

146

The Judge looks at Howard sadly. "I think I want to skip over this part, too," he says.

"Right," Howard agrees emphatically. "Well." He stops a minute, wondering how to continue.

"Go on, go on," the Judge prods.

Howard agrees unhappily, looking back at Eunice for a minute. "Well," he says finally, "when I went back to my room that night, she was taking a bath," Howard says. He looks at the Judge quizzically.

"No," the Judge decides after a moment. "Don't tell me. Let's skip it. Just go on with the story."

"Okay," Howard says, relieved. "Anyway, when Eunice walked in, the drapes caught on fire and everything burned, they asked me to leave the hotel. I really don't blame them," Howard says.

"Good boy," the Judge agrees, taking a slug of medicine straight from the bottle. "Is there more?"

"Oh, sure," Howard says.

"There's more," the Judge says sadly to the Bailiff. "All right, go on," the Judge tells Howard.

"The next day," Howard continues, "today, that is," he corrects himself, "Mr. Larrabee asked me to come to his house with my rocks and to bring Eunice—or rather, to bring Burnsy, the one he *thought* was Eunice. Is that clear?" Howard asks the Judge.

"No," the Judge tells him. "But it's consistent."

"Want me to go back over it?" Howard asks him.

"No. *No*—I beg of you. Please, just go on," the Judge pleads with Howard. The Judge reaches under the bench and takes out two large ball bearings from the drawer which he begins to roll around in his hand.

"Well," Howard continues, taking a deep breath, "at this point it got to be kind of complicated."

The Judge groans, and motions Howard to continue.

"First of all," Howard begins, "there was the trouble between me and Hugh."

147

"You and me?" the Judge says.

"No, not you. Hugh," Howard repeats.

"I am Hugh," Simon says, stepping forward.

"You are me?" the Judge says, baffled.

"No—I am Hugh," Simon repeats.

"*Stop saying that!*" the Judge yells. He turns to the Bailiff. "Make him stop saying that!" the Judge instructs the Bailiff.

The Bailiff takes a menacing step toward Hugh.

"Don't touch me," Simon says quickly, taking a backward step. "I'm a doctor."

"Of what?" the Judge asks, brightening noticeably.

"Of music," Simon says.

"Can you fix a hi-fi?" the Judge asks, a hopeful note in his voice.

"No, sir," Simon tells him.

"Then *shut up!*" the Judge yells.

The Bailiff moves Simon back with the others and then returns to stand near the Judge's bench.

"All right, Howard," the Judge says, "Go on."

"Anyway," Howard says, continuing his story, "he came in and tried to get my case." Howard turns around and points to Smith. "And then *he* came in," Howard explains, pointing out Jones to the Judge, "and tried to get his case." Howard points back to Smith. "And then they came in and tried to get all the cases and the shooting started," Howard says, singling out the hoods.

"They forced me to come with them," Harry now says quickly. "I was out in the car the whole time."

"You little fink!" Horatio begins moving in on Harry.

"He brought the stuff to us!" Tom says angrily to the Judge.

"That's right, Judge," Dick elaborates, pointing to Harry. "He fingered everybody."

The Judge raps on the bench for silence. Horatio

is stopped by a policeman before he reaches Harry.

"That's the one who struck me," Eunice yells angrily, pointing to Horatio.

"The man's a public menace," Larrabee adds.

"I fought like a tiger," Simon yells over the din.

The Judge is now pounding hard on the top of his bench, standing up and using all his strength. "Silence! Order!" he screams. "This is my last warning!" the Judge yells, and brings down the gavel again.

The bench breaks in half. The Judge looks at it sadly and settles back into his chair, his face angry.

The noise of the desk breaking has restored order to the court. Slowly the Judge rises to his feet, drawing his robe around him. His voice is calm, and he is once again in control of his courtroom.

"I am going to get to the bottom of this web of deceit and confusion if it takes me the rest of my life," the Judge warns, throwing a pill into his mouth. "And that may be any moment," he adds sadly.

"Now," the Judge continues, *"you!"* He points a finger at Judy, who has remained quiet throughout the proceedings. "You in the blanket," the Judge continues, glaring. "You seem to have caused all of this. Exactly what have you got to say for yourself?" the Judge demands.

Slowly, Judy extricates herself from the blankets, and then throws the blanket back off her head.

The Judge stares at her with his mouth slowly falling open.

"Hello, daddy," Judy says to the Judge.

Silently the Judge mouths her name, before he falls back into his chair.

The broken desk collapses around him.

CHAPTER TEN

A taxicab pulls up to the front door of a terminal at the San Francisco International Airport. Howard Bannister steps out, pays the driver, and slowly walks through the door into the terminal. Overnight case in hand, Howard makes his way to the center of the huge room, stopping and looking up at the arrival and departure board above the information booths. He is early for his plane. He looks around for a coffee shop, notices a sign pointing toward a corridor, and begins walking across the terminal's waiting room in that direction.

"Howard!"

Howard turns toward the door of the terminal, stops in his tracks, and stares at Judy, who is coming through the automatic door. Surprised, Howard puts his overnight case down on the floor and waits for her. Judy winds her way around several groups of people, carrying her overnight case, and makes her way toward Howard. When Judy finally reaches Howard, she stands and looks up at his face, silent. Howard looks at her, resigned.

"You got your rocks back," Judy says finally, pointing to his overnight case on the floor.

Howard nods. "You got your—things—back," he says, pointing to her case.

She nods.

They stare at each other without talking.

"Are you going somewhere?" Howard asks finally.

"Back to school," Judy tells him.

"Another one?" Howard asks.

"Sure," Judy says. "According to a nineteen-seventy study, there are about one thousand one hundred and forty-five institutions of higher education. I've got quite a few to go." Judy stops and peers over Howard's shoulder in the direction of the information booth. "Say, look who's here," she says.

Howard turns around to take a look, and they move over toward the information booth.

Fritz, carrying a suitcase and wearing a false moustache, is leaning toward the information girl.

"Please," Fritz is asking, "can you give me information about flights to Rio de Janeiro?"

The girl fumbles under the counter, and then hands Fritz a schedule booklet. Fritz takes it, quickly turns to leave the counter, and sees Howard and Judy, who are approaching. Fritz raises a hand to stop them, pauses, gives them a slick bow and heel click, and quickly looking around he turns and goes off toward the ticket booths.

Judy and Howard watch him go.

"It wasn't all so bad, was it?" Judy asks now. "I mean—of course, it was terrible that they took the grant away from you . . . ."

"Oh, they had to do that," Howard interrupts. "After all, the Larrabee Foundation just isn't used to having to bail their founder out of jail." Howard's voice trails off, a wistful note in it.

"Look," Judy tells him quickly. "There are a lot of other grants, you know. I was reading the other day

151

about a special award for musical research that the Juilliard School . . . ."

"Please, Judy," Howard says, stopping her. "Don't tell me about it. You have a way of making all these things sound reasonable. Then rooms start burning down and people start chasing people . . . ."

"Hey," Judy interrupts, pulling at Howard's sleeve. "Look at that," she says.

Howard looks over toward the doors, where Judy is pointing.

The golf bag over his shoulder, Jones has come through the automatic door into the airport terminal's lobby. The overnight case of documents is in his other hand, firmly attached to his wrist by a chain and lock.

Judy and Howard wave, but Jones does not see them.

A few seconds later, Smith comes through the same door. He is wearing a hat low over his forehead, and is walking stealthily, obviously stalking Jones. He is carrying a huge pair of wire clippers beneath his trench coat.

Judy laughs. Howard does not.

"I guess I owe you twenty thousand bucks," Judy tells Howard after a moment.

"Oh, don't be silly," Howard says.

"Listen," Judy says quickly, "if I paid you off at ten dollars a week, we'd be even in—uh—thirty eight years and five and a half months."

"Say, you did that fast," Howard observes.

"I took New Math at Mount Holyoke," Judy explains.

"Miss Maxwell!"

Howard and Judy look back to the door at the front of the terminal. Followed by a Brinks guard, who is carrying her overnight case, Mrs. Van Hoskins

152

is walking toward them. She is wearing a mini skirt and see-through blouse.

"Mrs. Van Hoskins," Howard says. "Hello."

"Hello, young man." Mrs. Van Hoskins turns back to Judy. "Miss Maxwell," she says, "as you may know, there was a twenty thousand dollar reward for the return of my jewels."

Howard and Judy look at each other.

"Twenty thousand," Judy says in an excited voice. "Wow!" She smiles happily at Howard.

Mrs. Van Hoskins opens her purse, with Judy and Howard staring at her.

"Now," Mrs. Van Hoskins says, pulling out a piece of paper and unfolding it. "I paid for the damage to your room, young man," she says to Howard. "That was twenty eight hundred dollars. The little car you drove into the bay, that was twenty four hundred dollars." Mrs. Van Hoskins is reading from her list. "The other two cars? The taxi was thirty four hundred dollars, and two thousand six hundred for the other."

"The other?" Howard asks.

"The convertible," Judy says.

"Yes," Mrs. Van Hoskins agrees.

"What else is there?" Howard asks.

"The pane of glass that was broken," Mrs. Van Hoskins continues, "that was sixteen hundred. Damages to the costume store, a restaurant, a delivery cart and, goodness me," she says, looking up for confirmation, "a Chinese dragon?"

Judy and Howard nod silently.

"Yes," Mrs. Van Hoskins continues, "well, that added up to thirty eight hundred fifty dollars. The canopy was two thousand, three hundred."

"Is that all?" Judy asks.

Mrs. Van Hoskins checks her list again. "Oh, and court costs, one thousand dollars," she adds. "That makes a grand total of nineteen thousand, nine hundred and fifty dollars, leaving fifty dollars to be split between you two, the cabdriver, that nice old man and the gentleman from the government." Mrs. Van Hoskins puts the list back in her pocketbook and extracts her wallet. She opens it and fumbles in the bill compartment.

"Here you are, and God bless you." Mrs. Van Hoskins hands a ten dollar bill to Howard, and one to Judy.

They look at the bills in their hands as Mrs. Van Hoskins walks off, trailed by the Brinks guard with her overnight case.

Judy hands her ten to Howard. "Hey," she says. "That leaves only thirty eight years, five months and a week to go," she says.

Howard laughs.

"See," Judy says, "sometimes it's kind of fun."

"Yes, I know," Howard agrees, serious again, "but. . ."

"Don't tell me," Judy interrupts. "You need peace and quiet."

"That's right," Howard agrees.

Suddenly Judy, too, is serious. "You'll miss me," she tells Howard quietly.

"I know that too," Howard agrees.

"Well . . ." Judy says.

"Well . . ." Howard says.

On an impulse, Judy puts her hand out. Howard takes it and holds it in his.

"*Howard!* Howard Bannister!"

Howard and Judy turn around.

Eunice is coming toward them, Frederick Larrabee at her side, and followed closely by Hugh Simon, who is carrying a suitcase and looking very pleased with himself.

154

"Eunice," Howard says. "What are you doing here?"

"We've come to see Mr. Simon off," Larrabee explains. "I'm sorry about what happened, Howard. I'm sure you understand."

"Absolutely," Howard says.

Howard and Larrabee shake hands.

"No hard feelings, eh, Bannister?" Simon asks.

"No, no," Howard assures him.

"*C'est la vie*," Larrabee says.

"*C'est la guerre*," Simon adds.

"*C'est la drek*," Judy says.

"Well," Simon says, "I'll be getting my plane now. So it's *arrividerci* to all."

"Don't forget this, Simon," Larrabee says quickly. He pulls an envelope from his pocket and extracts a check from it, which he hands to Simon. Simon looks at it hungrily, puts down his suitcase and takes the check from Larrabee. He looks at it for a long moment, licking his lips.

"Like to take a look at it, Bannister?" Simon asks finally. He holds out the check to Howard.

"It's very nice," Howard says.

"You deserved it, Howard," Eunice tells him sadly. "You really did."

"Well," Simon says hastily, "there are some, I suppose, who think there is some merit in the study of prehistoric mineral poundings, but I think the Hugh Simon theory of Swiss scale patterns will stand the test of time." Simon waves the check in the air.

"Just what is that theory?" Judy asks him.

"Well," Simon tells her, "I don't know that you're qualified to understand it, Miss Maxwell, but, briefly, the Simon theory advances the notion that the sixteenth and seventeenth century Swiss composers developed a unitonic scale pattern based upon the uniform intervals utilized in the mountaineer's yodel."

"You developed this theory?" Judy asks Simon.

"I invented it," Simon tells her.

"Then I guess that will come as some shock to Professor Findelmyer," Judy tells Simon sweetly.

"What?" Simon turns ashen. "What are you talking about?" He stares at Judy, horrified.

Larrabee, Eunice and Howard look at Judy and then at Simon.

"You know what I mean," Judy prods. "The Findelmyer proposition."

"Findelmyer?" Simon says, cringing. "I don't know what you're talking about."

Larrabee is looking at Judy with great interest now.

"Sure you do," Judy says to Simon.

"I do not!" Simon insists loudly. "Besides that has never been translated. . . ." Simon stops suddenly, realizing that he has tripped himself.

"Just once," Judy says, turning to explain the situation to Larrabee. "In nineteen twenty five, by the Harvard Press Musicological Review. It's probably out of print *now*, but if you . . . ."

"*Of course!*" Larrabee exclaims. "Professor Hevdrick Findelmyer. University of Zurich. In nineteen eleven. The controversial Findelmyer theory! No wonder it sounded so familiar!" Larrabee takes Judy's hand and shakes it happily. "Sorry, Simon," he says, turning back. Larrabee plucks the check out of Simon's hand and tears it into pieces.

"This is unspeakable!" Simon rages.

"Simon," Larrabee says, "you're a plagiarist. And what's worse—you're a bad loser. And you're nasty. I don't like you, and I want you to go away."

Breathing hard, and purple with rage, Simon picks up his suitcase and stalks off, cursing to himself in Croation. They watch him go.

"Howard," Larrabee says. "The Foundation will

156

make out a new check and send it off to you at the Conservatory. I am really very glad."

Howard smiles happily. "Thank you, Mr. Larrabee," he says simply.

"Frederick," Larrabee says. Larrabee takes Eunice by the arm. "And Howard," Larrabee continues, "I want you to know that I've asked Eunice to stay on with me here for a few days."

"In separate quarters," Eunice adds quickly.

"Of course," Howard says.

"We've shared a great deal in the past day or so," Larrabee explains. "I think, perhaps, well—you know what I mean," Larrabee finishes lamely.

"Good-bye, Howard," Eunice says. "You'd better hurry now or you'll miss your plane." Eunice is looking at the big clock on the arrival/departure board. "Come, Frederick," she continues. "It's twelve thirty five and the lecture starts promptly at one." Eunice pulls Larrabee away. Larrabee turns and waves at Howard.

Howard waves back, and watches them go.

"Well, Judy," Howard says, turning back, "I guess. . . ." Judy is not there.

"Judy?" Howard turns completely around.

"Judy!" Howard yells. She is gone.

Slowly Howard picks his overnight case up from the floor and dejectedly he heads for the boarding area where passengers are already entering the airplane.

Howard hands his ticket to a stewardess, and is seated near a window.

The seatbelt sign flashes on, the plane slowly taxis away from the airport onto the runway, and then smoothly takes off.

Glumly, his overnight case on his lap, Howard looks out the window at San Francisco, which grows smaller and smaller beneath him as the plane gains altitude.

In the front of the plane, the movie screen is down and the in-flight movie begins, with a Bugs Bunny Loonie Tune. Bugs Bunny and Elmer Fudd are singing. Howard looks away from the screen, suddenly depressed.

"I beg your pardon. What? No, I'm a transfer student."

Howard slowly straightens up in his seat, his eyes widening. It is Judy's voice.

"No. Not the University," Judy is saying. "The Conservatory of Music. It's in Ames. You've never heard of it?"

Slowly, a smile starts on Howard's face, as he carefully puts his overnight case down on the floor at his feet and unbuckles his seat belt.

"Well, it's a small conservatory," Judy is saying, "but there are those who love it. There's a professor there whom I hope to be studying with, a brilliant man, Howard Bannister. No—Bannister—as in sliding down the. You've never heard of him? Yes, that's right, the nut with the rocks."

Slowly Howard turns around, gets on his knees and cautiously peers over the back of his seat.

Judy is carrying on her animated conversation with an old lady who has her earphones on and is watching the cartoon, not paying a bit of attention to anything Judy is saying.

Howard slides over into the aisle seat, and adjusts it so it leans back all the way. He stares silently at Judy, who is sitting in the window seat, smiling at him happily.

"What's up, Doc?" Judy says.

"Did you happen to know that I love you?"

"Sure," Judy tells Howard, interrupting.

"You did?" Howard says. "Do?"

"Listen kiddo, you can't fight a tidal wave." Judy leans forward and, in the space between the seats, they kiss.

"About those things I said," Howard explains, "I mean—the way I acted back there. I'm sorry."

"Let me tell you something," Judy says meaningfully. "Love means never having to say you're sorry."

Howard looks at her strangely. "That's the dumbest thing I've ever heard," Howard says finally.

Judy nods happily; and slowly, leaning forward toward her, Howard returns Judy's smile.

THE BIG BESTSELLERS
ARE AVON BOOKS!

Inside The Third Reich Albert Speer	M107	$1.95
Zelda Nancy Milford	J113	$1.50
One Hundred Years Of Solitude Gabriel Garcia Marquez	J106	$1.50
Fire Island Burt Hirschfeld	W206	$1.25
Cindy On Fire Burt Hirschfeld	W261	$1.25
Between Parent & Child Haim Ginott	W139	$1.25
Between Parent & Teenager Haim Ginott	W234	$1.25
Sow Not In Anger Jack Hoffenberg	W126	$1.25
House On The Strand Daphne Du Maurier	W212	$1.25
The Flame And The Flower Kathleen E. Woodiwiss	J122	$1.50
Science Fiction Hall Of Fame Robert Silverberg, Ed.	J115	$1.50
Christy Catherine Marshall	W128	$1.25
Hard Times Studs Terkel	J109	$1.50
Throne Of Saturn Allen Drury	J127	$1.50
Never Leave Me Harold Robbins	N314	.95
The Arrangement Elia Kazan	J116	$1.50